One Grave Too Many

Ross Chisenhall lies defenceless and defeated as four riders viciously kill his only son. In time he recuperates from near-mortal wounds, but he is left not only with a scar on his face, but a darkness inside that cannot be quenched until his child's death is avenged. Under an assumed name he escapes to the town of Mesilla, where he soon discovers that he can be as cruel and brutal as the most savage gunman – and finally gets his chance to show that those four men dug one grave too many.

One Grave Too Many

Matt Cole

A Black Horse Western

ROBERT HALE

© Matt Cole 2020
First published in Great Britain 2020

ISBN 978-0-7198-3097-6

The Crowood Press
The Stable Block
Crowood Lane
Ramsbury
Marlborough
Wiltshire SN8 2HR

www.bhwesterns.com

Robert Hale is an imprint
of The Crowood Press

The right of Matt Cole to be identified as
author of this work has been asserted by him
in accordance with the Copyright, Designs and
Patents Act 1988

Typeset by
Derek Doyle & Associates, Shaw Heath
Printed and bound in Great Britain by
4Bind Ltd, Stevenage, SG1 2XT

Because I could not stop for Death –
He kindly stopped for me –
The Carriage held but just Ourselves –
And Immortality.
We slowly drove – He knew no haste
And I had put away
My labor and my leisure too,
For His Civility –
We passed the School, where Children strove
At Recess – in the Ring –
We passed the Fields of Gazing Grain –
We passed the Setting Sun –
Or rather – He passed us –
The Dews drew quivering and chill –
For only Gossamer, my Gown –
My Tippet – only Tulle –
We paused before a House that seemed
A Swelling of the Ground –
The Roof was scarcely visible –
The Cornice – in the Ground –
Since then – 'tis Centuries – and yet
Feels shorter than the Day
I first surmised the Horses' Heads
Were toward Eternity –

Emily Dickinson, 1890

BOOK 1

ONE GRAVE TOO MANY

CHAPTER 1

TO DIG ONE'S OWN GRAVE

The grave was basically dug when the four riders breached the knoll. Four dusty, hot men on saddle-worn horses, guns draped low on their hips, hats yanked down snug against the spitting mid-afternoon precipitation.

The sole surviving child – a boy – who dug the grave with his father, wept. His weeping was scarcely noticeable above the heart-rending scrape of the shovel skidding into the insipid New Mexico soil, the sporadic crash of unsympathetic thunder, the continuous clopping of the strangers' horses as they approached.

The boy's father, Ross Chisenhall, heard the horses, scanned out over the edge of the close dug grave, and saw the approaching riders. Chisenhall's face was fervent, bespattered by blood-covered dirt, a face that could have been carved in stone.

The riders were edging down the knoll, advancing towards the graves, one of which was still being dug.

Graves. The word was perverse in Ross Chisenhall's mind, like an impaled serpent. Graves. We all will end up in one, someday, he thought to himself. Yet he had already buried his little girl, Katy, and now he was working to bury his wife. Both six feet down, dirt on top, worm food. The bitter pain, momentarily abandoned, came back to gnaw at him.

He looked at the crude box that held her. Just the day before she had been alive, breathing, and he had shared a warm bed with her, the two had talked in low tones about the loss of their only daughter, their oldest child, just a few days before. And now . . .

'I'll be fine, Ross, stop fussin' over me,' Caroline had said. But that very night she had deteriorated, and then the coughing fits had took her over, and her voice had sounded as if she'd been in the creek trying to speak to him from beneath its water. And then . . .without warning and so suddenly . . .she had died.

Now she was rigid in an awful excuse for a coffin, going six feet below the taciturn, damp ground of a dreary December – and now the riders came. Uninvited. Poorly timed.

Chisenhall looked at his son, Johnny. He had been named after his grandfather. The boy was oblivious of the riders approaching. He stood on the grave bottom picking rocks from the soil with his shovel and at times with his hands. He knew only the sound and movement of the tool and the dirt; the wetness of tears and rain covered his round face.

Eleven and crushed, thought Ross Chisenhall. Shouldn't ought to be like this. Not for a boy his age.

And now the riders, about to pass by or through the haze of their sorrow. It did not seem decent or right; didn't seem right that the world went on; that boys should be motherless and husbands widowers.

It was all like a nightmare. All like a depressing, awful nightmare.

The riders were extremely close now.

Chisenhall looked at the crude coffin again. Waiting. If he had only had time and/or the money to build or buy her a proper coffin. But the weather was getting worse and the ground would only get harder, making burial near impossible.

The weather had no compassion, not one bit, for the dead.

Chisenhall pushed the shovel in the dirt and leaned on it, looked at the riders, and said without looking at the boy, 'Johnny, you get yourself inside the house, you hear?'

But Ross Chisenhall, blinded and anesthetized with heartache, had been too deliberate. Now the men were at the graves, looking down from the elevation of their horses, and very rudely, they were grinning.

'Come on back, junior, no need to run off 'cuz of us,' the foremost rider said, easing his horse even closer to the edge of Caroline Chisenhall's grave, leaning over the animal's neck and looking down on Ross and the growing pit of the grave. 'I find it a bit rude of ya, boy.'

Johnny stopped and looked to his father. Ross nodded, and the boy stopped. He let his hands nonchalantly find the hilt of the shovel. He had let go of it for an instant after the rider had addressed him, but now the hold of it felt safe again – not that he thought it would do much good against four fully grown and armed men, but it was at least something.

'What's in the box?' the leader of the four men asked, motioning his head toward the box that held the body of Ross Chisenhall's wife. 'Something ugly?'

'Sure is an ugly box,' laughed one of the other men.

'My wife died,' Chisenhall said easily. He flung a humorless look at Johnny out of the corner of his eye. His son was observing him, but his hands were clasping and loosening in quiet wrath.

The man – the leader of the four – wore a Confederate forage cap, though it had seen better days. The rest of his attire did not appear to be that of a Confederate soldier. A long artillery sabre hung at the man's right side, and a flap holster was on his right hip, the butt of a revolver peering out. It looked to be one of the old Confederate revolvers.

Under that grubby cap – maybe it had once been gray – was a face of identical grubbiness, the amused teeth standing out

9

in his mouth like the decaying remnants of wetland logs. There were several mutilations across the man's face, traversing from one side to the other.

Calmly, Chisenhall took in the three men with him. The first was rather young with a square jaw. He had two different colored eyes: one was blue and the other brown. The expression on his face was that of boredom. He had two pistols, one on each hip, and was dressed in dark but dusty clothing.

The second man was older, the same bored looked on his face as the younger man. He had a hint of a gray growth of a beard. He wore only one revolver – that Chisenhall could see – but it was distinctive, with its silver finish and pearl-white butt.

The third had a mouth full of tobacco and a half-mouth smile that allowed the tobacco juice to run down his chin and on to his neck. He was dressed entirely in black, was a bit over-weight, and appeared shorter than the other three.

'Mustn't have cared too much for your wife, putting her in an ugly crate like that,' the scarred-face man said.

'I cared a great deal for her,' Chisenhall replied quietly.

'Yeah, I can see that. What'd she do to deserve such harsh treatment like this? I wouldn't put my worst enemy in a pine box that looked as bad as that 'un.' The leader of the foursome looked back over his shoulder at his companions and smiled.

'If you say so,' Chisenhall replied.

'Daddy!' Johnny shouted.

'Be quiet now, Johnny,' Ross Chisenhall snapped.

The boy's mouth opened, worked, closed silently. But his hands still worked, grasping and loosening on the shovel's handle.

'Me and the boys here was wonderin' if mebbe you was burying somethin' besides your ugly wife in that ugly crate? Mebbe money or gold?'

'Don't be ridiculous,' Chisenhall chided the man. 'Do I look like a man with a crate of gold or money? Now off with you, I'm tryin' to bury my wife.'

10

'You ain't bein' right neighborly, mister,' the scarred rider said.

'Look . . .' Chisenhall began.

'No, you look,' the scarred man interrupted. 'I think we oughta take a looksey inside that crate of yours to make sure it ain't nothing more than the body of your wife.'

'Please leave me and my son alone.'

'Beginnin' to think you may be right, Ben,' the man with the mouth of tobacco said. 'There probably ain't no body in there at all.'

'There is,' Johnny cried.

'Leave us alone,' Chisenhall snapped.

'Mister,' the scarred man – Ben – said, 'You two ought to learn to be more hospitable to strangers. Folks have got to treat each other with respect.'

'All we want to do is to finish burying my wife, please,' Chisenhall pleaded.

'Mister, I ain't feelin' too much respect from you or your boy,' Scarface said.

Ross Chisenhall looked at the other men, hoping against hope that they could talk their leader into just riding off. But they looked at him, still grinning, the rain running in rivulets off the brims of their hats.

Ben, the scarred man, climbed down from the roan, walked over to the makeshift coffin. 'Now, I'm a gonna open this ugly box, and I'm a'gonna either use the end of your shovel, or your head. Choice is yours. Now, hand it up to me.'

It was at that moment Johnny made a move. He had grabbed up his shovel and started swinging it wildly in anger as he rushed the scarred man. The man jumped over the initial swing, which would have hit him in his knees if he hadn't. The next swing he caught with his left boot, stepping down on the middle of the shovel's handle and putting his weight on it, snapped it in half. Then in a flash his artillery sabre was unsheathed, and in one swift, precise thrust he drove the blade

11

into Johnny's stomach and out his back.

'NOOOO!!!' Ross Chisenhall screamed.

'Woo,' Scarface shouted. 'Straight through the boy. Looks like we're gonna be needin' another grave, mister.' He had turned to face Chisenhall.

The other three men were off their horses now, guns drawn.

'Don't go thinkin' you're some sort of hero, mister,' Scarface said. 'As we check out the contents of this ugly crate, you best start diggin' another grave for your boy.'

Ross Chisenhall screamed again.

'Better make that two more, one for yourself, too,' Scarface added.

Time was a blur. Chisenhall had dug two graves as ordered.

When he was done, he turned to face the four men. He was exhausted, physically and emotionally, yet he still had the fire to fight these outlaws.

And then his world exploded into a flash of bright and instant colors: white, red, and finally black – and not just black – complete darkness. Then he felt as if he were drifting into the air, floating away like a feather on the wind, all the way up as if he could reach out and touch a cloud.

Ross Chisenhall woke up in a mist of darkness, still weak, not clear, but hearing voices now.

'. . . Damn fool was tellin' the truth . . . ain't nothin' but the body of his wife in that ugly crate . . .'

Then he felt something sharp and painful in his shoulder. The scar-faced man had been standing over him and had stabbed him with his sabre. Maybe to see if he was dead or to finish him off, Chisenhall didn't know. Warm wetness on his shoulder and chest. Blood probably.

Chisenhall could no longer make out what the four men were saying. Flying away. Going to join his family: Caroline, Katy and Johnny . . .

CHAPTER 2

BACK FROM THE DEAD

The air was close and warm, heavy with moisture. Sweat and tears stung his eyes. The blackness was profound. The silence was worse. It was as silent as a tomb. He was buried, but not dead. No, he was able to move.

Dragging up his arm in the tightly enclosed space, he scraped against the hard surface about him, his breathing shallow.

He hurt like hell, but still he was able to move. His head seemed to be sticky and damp on his left side. That could be the result of his first wound, a bullet perhaps, but he had never heard it, only felt it, and it had sent him down. His thoughts raced. His face throbbed, and through the muddled areas of recollection, he recalled being struck while he was nearly unconscious and lost down in that world somewhere between restiveness and thoughts.

The fear then began to creep inside him. He started to tremble.

'Johnny,' he said aloud. 'Oh, Lord.' His voice was strange.

He reached out his hands to touch the darkness, they hurt

as if they had been trampled or smashed. Still they worked. He lifted the hand higher and it came to an abrupt stop. His fingers touched something hard, and then his fear turned into awareness. He felt something at his back. It was hard also, but irregular in shape.

Suddenly he knew. The terror was beyond his control as he kicked, thrashed, and yelled like a madman.

He had been buried alive, in a grave he had dug.

He began to shout, and to pound weakly in the limited space at the rocks and dirt piled over him.

Not a budge. He thought maybe he heard the slow sliding of dirt outside the grave, but he couldn't be sure. He took in a deep breath and relaxed. He tried to breathe shallowly and regularly, saving the air supply until he could come up with a plan. Provided there was any to come up with.

He lifted his right foot and touched the toe of his boot against dirt and rocks above him. Solid. Very damn solid in fact. He kicked swiftly.

One time. Twice. Once more.

Steady pace now. Kicking a little quicker, a little firmer. Both feet working now. Right. Left. Right. Left.

The dirt and rock began to break away ever so slightly, but it was breaking away.

Over and over.

Light began to shine through.

Firmer. Panicky. He no longer seemed to have the fear that a person would naturally expect under his circumstances. All he knew was that the grave was a lonely place and the silence of his tomb, which had been horribly oppressive, was becoming less frightening.

A rock fell on to his chest. He could feel it lying heavily there, making it harder to breathe.

He ceased kicking for a moment. Reached up and touched the rocks and dirt with the palms of his hands at chest level. He feared that more rocks and perhaps more dirt would suddenly crash down upon him.

The first sense of returning to life came over him when he saw the light from outside. He pushed harder, and soon his shoulders lifted him out of the grave and his head was hit by shifting rocks.

He was almost free. Writhing his fingers through the choking dirt, he began to work them upwards, scraping away the moist soil, curving his shoulders, pushing his way out.

Awareness began to spin again. He felt this time his visit to the land of the dead might be his last, but something inside him kept striving. Something darker even than death. Something black called vengeance.

He did not know how long it took him, but finally he worked his way upward. Above him was the moon, and the night was filled with cold.

He coughed out the dirt, gasped out loud, and fell to the ground, his lead lolling to the side as he glimpsed three more graves, two smaller than the other.

A tear rolled down his cheek, and then exhaustion took him. He stretched out on the cold ground and slept until strength returned and the cold brought him around.

He turned over on his back and stared at the moon. Then he worked himself up on one elbow. His family was gone. Ross Chisenhall bent his head and trembled intensely, and not from the cold. He cried great rivers. Cried himself dry for all time.

When he had wet the ground with his pain, grief and anger he felt strong again. He found one of the shovels and used it to stand.

He made his way into his house. Looking about, he could see that the four riders had ransacked it, probably looking for items to sell, or for money, or guns. Chairs and tables were turned over, some broken. The lamp that Caroline had loved so dearly was shattered. Flour and all manner of foodstuffs had been strewn about the kitchen. Devastation just for the sake of it.

15

He drew water from the well, took a dishcloth and cleaned himself up a bit. He dressed in clean clothes. Then he went out to the barn.

They had been there, too. The horses were gone, and so were some oats. The burro was still in its stall. Chisenhall watered and fed it, then he lit a lantern and went back to the graves, said his goodbyes.

When he was finished, he prayed silently. Then, kneeling over the grave of his wife, he said 'I'll be back when I've finished this, Caroline. Build you, Katy and Johnny proper coffins, lay you side by side. I swear I will.'

He then repeated words he had heard said at other funerals, or at least those he could remember, and returned to the house. One more night of sleep, on the floor, and then he would be off.

CHAPTER 3

THE RED ROSE GANG

A piece, they were worth five hundred dollars each, but together, as they were that hot Mesita del Gato, New Mexico morning, the four members of the Red Rose Gang were worth the grand sum of two thousand dollars dead or alive.

It was this knowledge that prompted Les Pardee, conductor of the El Paso-bound train, to do the foolish thing he did. Foolish because there were no valuables in the car worth more than a week's wage, and foolish because the Red Rose Gang were all notorious killers – men of the hardened outlaw breed who would kill as quickly as they would eat.

But two thousand dollars was two thousand dollars, and a man often left his brains behind when greed pointed the way for him.

'Git that there strongbox open, Rake,' said Ben Murchin, standing tall and menacing in the sunlit doorway of the car. The scar-faced man then added, 'We ain't got all day, boy.'

'Yes, sir, Mr Murchin,' Les Pardee said, fussing with the keys and thinking about the little derringer he kept in the strong-box for just such an emergency.

'Shake him up, Gus,' said massive Clem Darnell from the

opposite doorway, each hand on one of his twin revolvers.

The gang had daringly held up the train in a cutting along the border of New Mexico and Texas. A study of train movements had convinced the bad men that despite its proximity to the town, the cutting that concealed the train from the surrounding country was the ideal spot for a holdup. Even so, big Darnell was getting jumpy. There was law in El Paso. The worst kind, too – Texas Rangers.

Ben Murchin glanced toward the loco. He had taken care of the engineer and fireman with two quick shots, so there was no trouble likely from that quarter. Turning in the other direction, the slim silhouette of the gang's killer and boss was cast further down the train.

'Simmer down, Clem,' Ben Murchin drawled, scarred face moving in a grin. 'Go take a look at the horses. Boy blue here ain't gonna make no trouble, are you, boy blue?'

That was where Ben Murchin was wrong. As the sound of Darnell's big boots receded along the right-of-way, the strongbox lock snapped open. Les Pardee reached inside, not for the meager little bag of valuables, but for the sneak gun.

Had the conductor tried his little trick on Clem Darnell, he might have pulled it off. But though not as incredibly fast with a cutter as Ben Murchin, he was at least sharp-witted, and possessed a finely honed sense of danger that left many men behind. Murchin smelled Pardee's treachery even before the derringer appeared.

'Why, you sly little runt,' Murchin said almost admiringly before squeezing the trigger.

Pardee was killed by the first bullet, reeling back with arms flung out, the unfired derringer clattering from his fingers. But that wasn't good enough for Ben Murchin. Two more bullets coming hard on the heels of the first spun Pardee around and punched him clean out of the car.

Rake Hanley came running as Murchin dropped to one knee by the strongbox. Sparing not a glance for the dead guard, young Hanley called:

'What did we get, Ben?'

Murchin's face as he broke open the canvas bag told its own story.

'Peanuts! Some lousy bank papers and forty bucks!'

Hanley's jaw fell. Misfortune had been riding with them every mile of late. If they robbed a bank, its largest depositor had just withdrawn his last greenback. They held up a stage-coach . . .and found it was carrying two hundred pounds of prime steaks to a cattleman's convention in Las Cruces. They had heard that this train often carried gold dust and they had been relying heavily on it to replenish their coffers. Then there was the farmer and his boy . . .

Bad luck still dogged their every step.

'Riders comin'!'

'How many?' Murchin hollered, leaping down to the right-of-way.

'Ten, mebbe fifteen,' Gus Rourke called, leading the way at a run toward a spot where the horses were cached.

Rourke's second estimate proved to be much closer than the first, for on reaching Darnell and the horses, they had a glimpse of fourteen purposeful horsemen galloping dustily toward the cutting.

Ben Murchin cursed luridly as he swung into the saddle. There had been no alarm given from the train, he knew, but figured that it had been on a tight schedule. The moment it was overdue, these men had been sent out to investigate. Nor were they ordinary men. Though still beyond rifle range, Murchin's experienced eye read their sign, and there was an extra urgency in his spurs as he led the gang away at a gallop. Clem Darnell also identified the lean riders and their runty, iron-limbered mustangs.

'Kenyon, Ben?' Darnell asked, drawing level to Murchin's racing bay.

Murchin's answer was another blistering profanity. Any

mention of the famed outlaw hunter Captain Mike Kenyon was liable to evoke such a reaction from the outlaw, particularly these days when things were going so badly for them. Captain Kenyon had been given his assignment personally by the governor of Texas at the start of the year:

'Wipe out the outlaw bands that are making this state a stench to all law-abiding Westerners.'

High on that list, of course, if not at the very top, was the Red Rose Gang.

If that was Kenyon on his hammer back there, Murchin reflected bitterly, it was the third time in three short months that the ranger had flushed them out.

The outlaws discovered that their fears were well founded when late that night, after a gruelling chase northwest from El Paso, they clashed with their pursuers. It was Kenyon all right, and because it was the captain, Murchin lost no time in breaking off the engagement. A back trail that Rourke knew got them away – but far from clear. Dawn found them west of Harper's Springs, with Kenyon's rangers still a threatening blob of dust behind them.

CHAPTER 4

A WEAPON OF VENGEANCE

Before dawn Ross Chisenhall was up. He surveyed his head and face in Caroline's mirror, saw that the head wound on his left side was an abrasion, but nothing apparently too serious. The wound on his face was significantly deeper and had caked with blood. It was in the shape of a half moon, and there was no doubt in his mind that it would leave one hell of a scar, a scar that would continually remind him, a scar that reached to the pits of his soul.

At the basin he washed his face, cautious with his bruised left cheek, and then went to the bedroom and reached under the bed, and pulled out his .44 caliber single-action Smith & Wesson Model 3 six-shooter revolver from hiding. He unwrapped the gun belt from about the holster and strapped it around his waist. The last time he had worn it had been the day it had been given to him after he had buried his father. His father had worn it for the Confederacy during the War between the States, and Chisenhall had immediately removed it, having heard of the violence from his father. But now there would be more – this time of his own making – and he would enjoy it.

He turned, looked at his damaged face in the mirror.

The .44 caliber revolver flew into his hand and the mirror shattered into a rain of silver fragments and his ears rang from the shot.

His farm was behind him, nearly fifteen years in the making. It was now a distant memory. He was somewhat amazed that he could shoot at all. His first thought had been to charge out after the men, hunt them down and get his revenge. But he faced the fact that they were four, and for over fifteen years now he had been a farmer, not a pistol man.

Besides, their trail was already cold, and last night's rain had wiped away what sign there might have been – at least any sign he could follow. He had never been much of a hunter nor a tracker. But there was one thought that clung to Chisenhall: the outlaws had to pass through Mesita del Gato, and he just might be able to pick up their trail there, if he were lucky. And if not, well, he would find them even if they went to the ends of the earth. Better yet, they were not even aware that he was alive, that he was a man hard set on retribution, and that he would ride them down into the very dirt. At the moment he felt a half-day's practice would serve him significantly, and the other half day would bring him into Mesita del Gato. With some luck they would still be there. It was the only town within twenty miles, with a well-stocked saloon and a top-notch brothel.

Chisenhall felt it best to get to know and understand his weapon of revenge, as he cleaned it. The revolver had a plain walnut square butt, an irregular shaped side plate inserted from the left side, held in position with a hammer stud nut and two plate screws. The gear catch cut was in the bottom strap rear of the barrel joint with a blue finish and round body ribbed top, jointed to the frame at the bottom strap forward of the guard latching to the frame at the bolster interlocking frame post with the jointed barrel catch. The lug was raised from the body extending forward of the joint encasing the extractor spring and the round rack.

It had six chambers and was counterbored to receive the flanged head extractor with ratchet. There was a center hole for the extractor stem made square. The hammer was straight side, checked thumb piece, solid round pointed nose, slotted to receive the plain mainspring stirrup. It was hand pivoted to the left side; the handspring slot cut in the front face to receive the flat spring. It had a case-hardened finish. It was made of carbon steel, tempered.

A solid bow guard screwed to the frame, also with a case-hardened finish.

Time after time he loaded the revolver, and the countryside was filled with the sound of gunfire. Bottles shattered, rocks flew, fence posts fractured.

The dance of inanimate objects went on for a long while until he had very little ammunition left. Not long ago he would have considered this an extravagant waste, but now, in each bottle that shattered, in each rock that jumped, and in each post that he splintered, he saw the four faces of the murderers – the men who had disrupted the burial of his wife, killed his son, and left him for dead. Four to pay: one, two, three and four shots! The time would come for each of the four killers.

He went to the barn, saddled up the burro, packed a few belongings, including a bag of oats, and just before high noon, not a scrap of food in his belly, he set out for Mesita del Gato, the burro loping along as only animals of this sort can.

Just before dusk he came upon a campsite, that of the killers most likely, possibly from last night. He stopped long enough to have a drink, and long enough to fill his hat for the burro to drink. Then he was off again, the faces of the four killers everlastingly before him.

He thought of the bible, and the passage from Romans 12:19: 'Beloved, never avenge yourselves, but leave it to the wrath of God, for it is written, "Vengeance is mine, I will repay, says the Lord."'

Well, where was the Lord when they had killed little Johnny? Tell you this much, Lord, I am not avenging myself, but Johnny – they may not see your wrath, but they will feel my vengeance.

Not long after, just as the moon was soaring high above in the night sky, he arrived in Mesita del Gato.

CHAPTER 5

LOOKIN' FOR SOMEONE, ALL RIGHT

A chubby, brown-haired squawker of a lady was wrenching out another number to the melody of a scratchy piano plunked by an out-of-tune, intoxicated piano player. But they were the finest, because they were all there was at The Buzzard's Roost Saloon.

It wasn't the fanciest of saloons, but it had the basics: a bartender, glasses, spittoons and – most importantly – alcohol. A dozen cowboys, more used to the music than appreciating it, sat about in the indistinct light dealing cards, or sagging over their tepid beers or a bottle of coffin varnish.

Jack Lindsey, the bartender, sat behind the bar picking at a scab inside his nose. A drunken cowboy had crushed it very good a day before. He smeared the findings of his exploration on his already soiled smock.

A man dressed completely in black sat at the back of the saloon nurturing a beer and caressing the fleshy rear of a red-headed saloon girl who sat in his lap. He was attempting to talk her price down before he decided whether to take her upstairs to conclude the business transaction.

Outside the saloon, peeping now and then over the batwing doors, the resident town drunk, Dal Tanner, loitered and measured the parchedness of his gullet. He was watching for someone who might come along and offer to buy him a drink. No one had come by for nearly an hour now, and it looked to be a slow night. His prospects of getting a drink were slim. The place usually got crowded early if it got crowded at all.

He had thought extensively about the visitor in black – thought maybe he might talk him out of a coin. But from the airs of him, he didn't look like a man to be trifled with, as bad-tempered a looking fella as them that he had rode with in the past.

Dal brushed the back of his hands across his mouth. His lips were as dry as a desert. They were aching, too. He needed a drink direly, and . . .

He heard a rider coming close. Rotating, he saw a lanky man ride in on a burro, moving up the street in a slow, plodding fashion.

Something about the tall man caused Dal Tanner to be uneasy. Even at a distance it was noticeable, and it was with some wonder that Dal finally established the man as Ross Chisenhall, the farmer.

But he appeared unusual now, and that was an underestimation. Something was different. An internal fervor had been stoked and now Chisenhall looked extremely seared up with it. A profound, furrowed scar was on the left side of his cheek, and the way the moonshine hit it, made it all the poorer, made it look like a blood-covered curved blade.

Dal Tanner shivered at the sight.

Ross Chisenhall halted before the saloon and looked at Dal, or rather looked through him. He climbed down off the burro and tied it and walked up on the boardwalk. He did not converse with Dal.

Dal Tanner half nodded, turned, and walked down to the edge of the saloon and waited there quietly.

Chisenhall went in through the batwing doors, palming them aside with great force, walking forward with heavy clumps of his boots.

The chubby, brown-haired woman stopped in mid-squawk, turned to look at Chisenhall. The intoxicated piano player ceased to plunk at the keys. Cowboys stopped their card games in mid-deal or put their beer down in mid-drink.

The man who had come in looked plumb crazy, his eyes blazing like a brush fire.

Chisenhall disregarded them. He looked around.

The man in black had vanished.

Jack, the bartender, said, 'Comin' in here kinda loudly, aren't you?' Chisenhall disregarded him and went over to lean on the bar.

The female singer went back to squawking to the out-of-tune plunking of the piano.

The cowboys continued their games and their beers.

Jack Lindsey looked at Ross Chisenhall. He had known the man for a fair amount of years, but if not for the fact, he might have not recognized the man who stood before him now. And sporting a gun on his hip. He had never seen Chisenhall wear a gun before. Chisenhall's eyes looked awfully peculiar, like a man in disbelief. And the scar, it was profound and coated over with blood, painful looking.

'You lookin' for someone, Ross? God, man have you seen a doctor, about that?' Lindsey pointed to the scar. 'How'd it happen, Ross?'

Chisenhall paid the barkeep no attention, shrugging off his questions. 'I am lookin' for someone all right!'

'Yeah, and who is that? You know, Ross, you might ought to see the doc. I mean . . . that doesn't look good . . . .'

'Four no-account bastards who killed my son, buried me alive, humiliated the body of my dear Caroline.'

Jack Lindsey looked shocked. 'Caroline is dead? Johnny too? No, not after what happened to little Katy?'

'Johnny was murdered. Caroline died of the pox, same as Katy, least I guess she did. Sonofabitches that killed my son buried me alive.'

'Good Lord, Ross!' Lindsey exclaimed. 'I can't believe it.'

Chisenhall looked at the back table where a half empty beer mug sat. 'See any strangers come through here, Jack?'

The bartender bit his lip and looked at the beer mug. He liked Ross Chisenhall, but he didn't like trouble. But finally, 'Four men rode in here earlier, split up. Only one stayed, the other three rode away.'

Chisenhall stared at the beer mug. 'One that stayed?'

The bartender reduced his voice to a murmur. 'Just went upstairs with Maria.'

Chisenhall nodded. 'I reckon he will be a dead man soon.'

'Now, c'mon, Ross, I know you're foolishly angry, and you got every right to be. But you're no gunfighter, you're a farmer. This fella looks as mean as a rattlesnake . . .' Jack Lindsey stopped in midsentence. The man looking at him now, lips tight, eyes afire, looked just as mean as any rattlesnake he'd ever seen. Maybe meaner. 'I think – think mebbe you ought to wait and get the law in on this. That's the sheriff's job, Ross. Besides, you could have the wrong man, you think?'

'If he is the wrong man, he is lucky. If he is the right one . . .' Chisenhall looked at Lindsey '. . . he won't be as lucky.'

Jack Lindsey could not believe that it was the Ross Chisenhall he knew who was talking. The voice sounded so peaceful, cold even, emotionless, so eerie. Here Ross Chisenhall was, leaning on the bar, a half moon-shaped scar on his face, telling him as simple and calm as could be that four men had murdered his son, buried him alive and disgraced the body of his dead wife. Was telling him that he was going upstairs to kill a man, if he was one of the four.

Lindsey said, 'C'mon, let me go and get the sheriff, Ross.

Won't be but a sec.'

'What's he gonna do? He's a bigger drunkard than old Dal outside,' Chisenhall noted.

Jack was getting nervous now. 'It's his job, Ross.'

'No,' Chisenhall said as he shook his head. 'This is my job. Mine alone.'

'I just don't want to see you get hurt,' the bartender offered.

Chisenhall sneered, there wasn't much jollity in it. 'Or your saloon shot up, I reckon.'

'Well . . . that too . . . sure.'

Chisenhall sneered again, dreadfully frigid. 'What does this fella look like?'

Lindsey paused. 'Dressed in black, gray stubble of a beard . . .'

'Wears a pearl-handled revolver sticking out of his belt,' Chisenhall's voice began to get stronger with anticipation of seeing one of the four killers.

'Sounds about right.'

Without looking at Jack Lindsey, Chisenhall stood and said, 'I'll try to make this neat . . . and quick.'

'Ross . . .'

'You reach for that shotgun behind the bar, Jack, you're a dead man. Got no squabble with you, but I'm here to exact my ounce of flesh . . . I aim to kill that sonofabitch upstairs.'

Just as plain and simple as that – and Jack knew that if he pulled the shotgun Ross would make him use it. He could see that in the farmer's eyes. There would be no holding Chisenhall at gunpoint until someone brought the sheriff. No. Ross Chisenhall would go for his gun, and someone, maybe his bartending self, would be killed.

Jack Lindsey raised his hands. 'I won't touch it . . .I swear, Ross.'

Chisenhall nodded.

'Maria's up there, Ross,' Jack reminded him.

Nodding again, Chisenhall started for the stairs at the back of the saloon, the ones that led up to the overhead crib where the girls did their deeds.

'What room?' Chisenhall said back to the bartender softly, yet firmly.

Lindsey licked his drying lips.

'I will break every one of 'em down, Jack.'

'OK . . . Room 4.'

Chisenhall nodded. 'Fours are wild.' He went up the stairs.

Jack Lindsey stepped backwards slowly, slid out from behind the bar, and went for Sheriff Leach.

The music had stopped again, and the heavy woman who had been singing, the bad piano player, and all present had turned their attention to the upstairs portion of the building.

CHAPTER 6

DEAD MAN WALKING

Jack Lindsey scurried diagonally across the street to the sheriff's office, found the old man seemingly lifeless on one of his cell bunks. If not for the fact that the cell door was ajar, and a tin star was on the big, barrel-chested man's chest, he would have looked more like a drunken prisoner than a sheriff.

'Sheriff,' Jack yelled pulling at the old man's sleeve. 'Get up from there, c'mon now. Ross Chisenhall is fixin' to kill the hell out of a man.'

'What time – what are you sayin'?' the sheriff said in a big, deep voice as he rubbed sleep from his eyes.

'Get up, c'mon, move it before you're too late,' Jack urged.

'I'm a . . . I'm a comin',' the sheriff groaned.

'Over at the saloon. Ross Chisenhall. He is in a shock or somethin'. Talkin' about someone killin' his boy. He's got a gun, Sheriff.'

The sheriff batted his bloodshot eyes opened. 'Chisenhall, the farmer?'

'Yeah, Ross Chisenhall. Come on or it will all be over before you get off that bed,' Jack was anxious and tugged again on the sheriff's sleeve.

31

That was exactly what Sheriff Yale Leach was hoping for – to be honest. 'Let me see. Where did I leave my gun?'

'You're wearin' your gun, you darn fool, come on!'

'Yeah, so I am,' Leach said with a smirk, patting the butt of his revolver.

'Sheriff, come on, daggumit!'

Half hauling the big, wobbling Sheriff Leach, Jack Lindsey started back across the street. Leach worked hard to sober himself up, took his revolver from its holster and held it before him, hoping he could bluff his way out of this situation.

When Chisenhall reached Room 4 he didn't bother to draw his gun. He raised his foot and kicked the door open with a boom.

The man in black was no longer in black. His flabby, fleshy body was nude, and he was straddling the sought-after red-head, guns and dying the furthest thing from his mind. His clothes and revolver lay on the floor. When the door flew back and collided with the wall he rolled off the woman and hit the floor, seizing at this gun. The man was quick, very quick. He rolled, brought the gun up quick as a hiccup, levelling it at Chisenhall.

Chisenhall drew and fired.

His shot struck the man in the right shoulder and scooted him across the floor a full two feet. A gush of blood shot up and covered the man, the mattress and the woman, who was now squealing.

Chisenhall walked over to the man and leaned over him. The man kept trying to make his arm work, so he could pick up his gun, but no way was it going to work. The nerves and the bone were crushed. He looked up into the dark face of Ross Chisenhall, the scar on his left cheek was noticeable, but the look in his eyes was more evident.

Chisenhall dropped his face. 'Do you recognize me?'

'No . . . no . . .honest . . . I don't!'

'Just yesterday and you have already forgotten me . . . my boy . . .'

Recollection then crept over the wounded man's features. 'Oh . . . no . . . we . . . we . . .'

'Killed my boy,' Chisenhall said through gritted teeth. 'And buried me alive? Is that what you are trying to say?'

The man tried for the gun again. The arm was still dead, but he thought the small measure might distract the farmer, so he could reach over and pick up the gun with his other hand.

But Chisenhall had anticipated that. He put the toe of his boot on the man's left hand. He then said, 'You carry a knife, mister?'

The man shook his head in response.

Chisenhall smirked, reached over and picked up the man's clothes from the night stand and tossed then the plump red-head. 'Check those out to see if he is tellin' the truth that he doesn't have a knife.'

The naked woman nodded nervously and went through the clothes, tears and snot covering her face.

'I can't find one,' she blubbered.

'Well, don't that beat all,' Chisenhall said. 'I did not want to have to get blood on my knife.' He reached down into his boot and pulled out a long, shiny hunting knife.

'Go on, git, girl!' Chisenhall snapped at the red-head.

Maria stretched out for her clothes.

'Go on!' Chisenhall snapped again.

Maria, butt-naked, dashed for the door and the stair landing. Chisenhall hear her shout. 'Sheriff! Sheriff Leach! Sheriff!' That meant that big, old Yale Leach was inside the saloon.

Chisenhall could see the man gulp profoundly, could see the optimism in his eyes as the woman shouted. 'We're up here, Sheriff.'

Chisenhall shifted his foot so that he held the wrist, and then, putting weight on it, he bent and drove the knife into the man's left hand, trapping it to the wooden floorboard. The man shrieked more noisily than the woman had.

'It will take him some time to get up here,' Chisenhall noted.

He could hear the sheriff's heavy-set footfalls on the stairs now, not moving too swiftly, not anxious at all. He would be by himself, of that Chisenhall was sure of. The whole town was a bunch of sheep. Maybe he had grown just like them – that was, until the day before.

Leaving the man with his hand pinned to the floor, Chisenhall walked over to the door. 'You comin' up, Sheriff?'

The sheriff's head showed at the top of the stairs. Sweat was running down his hatless head and dripping down his reddened face.

'Tell . . . tell me . . . you didn't go and kill that man, Ross,' the sheriff gasped.

Chisenhall shook his head. 'Not just yet.'

The sheriff noted that Chisenhall still held his revolver in his hand.

'Am I goin' to need to use my gun against you, Ross? I would certainly hate to have to do that.'

'I would hate that too, Sheriff,' Chisenhall calmly replied. 'I don't want to kill you, Leach.'

'You messin' with me, or you shootin' straight?' The look on Leach's face revealed his wish of having chosen a better word than 'shootin'.

'Just hurry up and get on up here.'

Sheriff Yale Leach crossed the landing and walked on cautious feet to Chisenhall. 'I'll go ahead and have your gun now, Ross.'

'Oh,' Chisenhall said softly looking down at the revolver. 'Sure thing, Sheriff.' And with that Chisenhall pushed the barrel of the sheriff's pistol aside with one hand and slammed the side of his gun across the side of the big man's head, dropping him like a weighty sack of flour. 'Sorry, Sheriff . . . well . . . I just am.'

He next bent down and took Leach's pistol and stuck it in

34

his belt. He tied the big man's wrists with his own gun belt. When that was completed he walked over to the stair rail and peered down. A few uneasy faces met his stare.

'The sheriff said for you to all go back to your lives. Mind your own damn business. Understand me?'

The folks down below swapped looks with each other.

'Why doesn't the sheriff tell us hisself, then?' one man asked.

Chisenhall waved the man and the others off before disappearing.

'He's killed the sheriff too, I reckon,' Maria said. She was wrapped in one of the tablecloths, most of her still spilling out of it. However, at that time, no one was all that interested in her. Hell, most of the men had seen it all before, and her prices were getting lower by the year. Besides, what the tablecloth didn't cover, the blood did.

'What do we do now?' Jack Lindsey asked nervously.

One of the card-playing men shrugged nonchalantly. 'Whatcha mean, we, Jack? I don't have a dog in this fight. It's your place. You ought to be the one to go on up there.'

'What? Who me? No sir, not this fella,' Lindsey replied. 'Ross Chisenhall has lost his mind. I'm no fool to go runnin' up there.'

Dal, the town drunk, had used the confusion to slip inside the saloon. 'Ross ain't Ross anymore. Somethin' is wrong with 'im. It's like he's dead . . . you know . . . in the inside. He may be walkin', talkin' and shootin', but that is a dead man if I ever seen one.'

'What are you talkin' about, Dal?' the plump, squawker asked.

'I ain't never seen no dead man walk 'fore,' the card-playing man said. 'You're drunk, Dal.'

'Not as drunk as I'd like to be,' Dal noted. 'I looked Ross Chisenhall in the eyes and saw . . .' Dal burped before he could finish.

'What did you see?' Maria asked.

With one hand to his stomach and the other to his mouth, Dal Tanner looked like he might vomit. After a brief pause, he lowered the hand by his mouth and said, 'I saw nothin'. I'm tellin' you, it was like lookin' into the eyes of a man who just died.'

'Anyway,' the card-player said, 'he says that stranger in black killed his boy.'

'Can't fault a man for wantin' to kill a man who murders a young boy,' another of the men stated.

'That's up to the law to decide,' Jack Lindsey added.

The singer huffed. 'What law do we have? The old fat bull that waddled up the stairs a few minutes ago? He won't make much of a difference. Hell, bet Dal would make a better lawman than Leach.'

Dal Tanner smiled at the backhanded compliment.

'Maybe Leach is tryin' to talk Ross out of killin' that man,' the squawker said.

'Could be,' Dal replied. 'But . . . but . . . I would sure hate to be the man in black right about now.'

'Well, one thing is for sure,' Maria said, 'He ain't all in black now.'

When Chisenhall left the stair railing, he went back to room four and took a seat on the bed's edge. The man was still squirming, trying to pull the knife out of his hand, but his free hand was covered in blood, making it hard to grip the knife's handle. He could not free himself.

'I'm goin' to bleed to death,' the man shouted. 'That want you want?'

'I wouldn't complain if you did,' Chisenhall replied without emotion.

'C'mon, you won't let me die like this will ya, covered in blood and naked?'

'Reckon I could,' Chisenhall said folding his legs over each other.

'It wasn't me who killed your boy, or buried you in that grave, I swear on my mother's name,' the men pleaded.

'You watched them do it. You didn't try to stop them. You were there.'

'But I didn't want to be a part of all of that, I promise you.'

'That so?'

'That is so. I swear it!'

'Why didn't you stop them then?'

'Really, I wanted to, I did. Honest. But then they would have just killed me too.'

'So now I kill you.'

The man just stared at Chisenhall and saw that the farmer from the day before was not the same man who spoke to him now.

'For the love of God, please! It wasn't me that did those things to you or your boy!'

Chisenhall nodded. 'Where are the other three? Why did you all split up? Where can I find them?'

Chisenhall repeated himself slowly when the man did not answer. 'Where are the other three men? Why did you leave them? Where am I going to find them?'

'I don't know. We just decided to split up. No particular reason why. Look, I'm goin' to bleed to death before I can answer your questions.'

'Tell me,' Chisenhall said. 'Why did you all split up?'

'We never got along very well, that's the truth of the matter.'

'This is the last time I will ask politely. Where are the others? Why did you leave them?'

The man was full out bawling now. 'I'm tellin' you. We didn't get along all that well. We didn't like each other. We came into some money and decided to spend some time apart. They went their way and I went my own.'

The blood was starting to pool around the man's hand and up around his shoulder.

'Tell me where I can find them.'

The short and somewhat chubby man sounded a bit different, Chisenhall noted, without a mouthful of tobacco. 'The youngest one – the kid – I don't know. I swear it. I don't know. Rake, he. . . .'

Chisenhall perked up – he had a name. 'Rake?'

The naked man pinned to the floor with a knife gave in. 'Rake Hanley. He went to Mesilla. It's over near a place called Antony, not far from a hole in the road called Santo Grande.

'And I should take your word as gospel?'

'I swear to the Lord Almighty.'

'You'd swear to anything, you no account, low down piece of filth,' the voice wasn't so peaceful now.

'I've told you the truth – what I can tell; pull out this knife, please! Get me a doc, for the love of God!'

Chisenhall did not move, he wasn't through with his questions. 'You fellas split this money from a robbery?' Before the naked man could answer, Chisenhall kicked him in the ribs. 'I asked you a question.'

'Yes, yes . . . we did. We robbed the Akela Springs Bank. Oh, God, I'm hurtin' real bad here. C'mon, help me!'

Ross Chisenhall just looked at him emotionless.

'For the love of all that is holy, good Lord man, get me a sawbones!' the bleeding man begged.

'What would be the point of that?' Chisenhall asked as he cocked back the hammer of his revolver, and pointed it at the man's head.

The man did not have a chance to spew any further pleas of mercy.

Everyone below the room recoiled when the shot was heard.

CHAPTER 7

NEVER SPOKE TO A DEAD MAN BEFORE

When Chisenhall came down the steps, the smoldering .44 caliber single-action Smith & Wesson Model 3 six-shooter revolver in his hand, the stranger's and the sheriff's revolvers slipped neatly in his waist belt, no one made a move to prevent him from leaving.

'After I leave,' Chisenhall said, laying his own pistol on the wooden bar, 'I would be obliged if one of you fine folk would go upstairs and release Sheriff Leach. I don't care what you do with that other lousy piece of filth – you can leave 'im, or toss 'im in the street and leave 'im for the buzzards for all I care.'

The people who were around him said nothing and stared blankly at him.

No one dared to move.

The red-head was still wrapped – and poorly so – in the tablecloth, and still blood covered. Chisenhall said to her as he placed some coins in her hand: 'Here is what you would have earned from that fella, the rest is mine from what he and his boys took from my house.'

Next he turned to Dal. 'They took both of my horses, and

I'm guessin' they sold them, and although I am certain that none of you fine folk knew they'd been stolen, even though some of you know my stock . . . anyways . . . Dal, I would like it if you ran across to the livery and found this fella's horse. I reckon I will be takin' it as mine now.'

Dal Tanner smacked his somewhat dry lips, but stood there.

'C'mon, get a movin'!' Chisenhall said resolutely.

Dal spun, pushed his way through the batwing doors, and vanished.

'This fella's partners are gonna be comin' after you, Ross,' Jack Lindsey said.

Chisenhall nodded. 'Uh-huh, I reckon they will.'

'There shouldn't be a law against killin' fellas like this polecat,' Maria said as she smiled at Chisenhall. 'And if any of us had known they had your horses or what they'd done, you can bet we'd have said something. Don't see nothing but the inside of this dirty saloon most days.'

'I bet any one of you would've, uh-huh,' Chisenhall said sarcastically.

The small group waited, quiet. Dal reappeared at the saloon doors after a few moments. 'I got the horse just as you . . . um . . . asked, Ross. It's saddled and ready for you.'

'I doubt I'll be seein' any of y'all any time soon,' Chisenhall said. He went out through the batwings, not bothering to say another word or to give any of them another glance.

Dal Tanner was standing on the boardwalk, smacking his lips, his tongue swishing back and forth across his teeth like a horse's tail brushing away flies. 'Obliged,' Chisenhall said handing him a handful of coins. 'Go quench your thirst, Dal.'

'Ross, thank you, thank you!' Dal nearly shouted.

'You can keep my mule, do with it what you want. I won't be needing him any longer.'

'Sure, Ross,' Dal began. 'There's a might lot of bullet in them saddlebags, some jerky, and a bottle of rye too.'

Chisenhall was silent, but nodded his acknowledgement,

turned the horse with ease, and headed east. East, the direction of Mesilla, and a murdering polecat named Rake Hanley.

As he rode off in a bolt, Dal clasped the coins in his hand, and spat into the dirt. 'I've never spoken to a dead man before.'

That he was now a wanted man did not bother Ross Chisenhall. He seemed beyond feeling. But that night as he camped beneath the night sky filled with twinkling stars, the exertion of being beaten, stabbed, shot and buried alive, and clawing his way up out of a hole in the ground; the emotional impact of burying, in a span of less than a week, his two children and his wife; the fact that he had practically not slept at all – all this had built up to kill any resemblance of a man; it all caught up with him, and he passed out. It was not a peaceful slumber, but it was sleep nonetheless.

His dream fell back a few years and he could see Caroline swollen with child, her face bright, dreams lighting up her eyes like wildfires. Falling back even more, the construction of their home, even as far back as cutting the timber for the wood, the creation of their goal – a piece of land to call their own. A place to raise their children. He stopped his thoughts – the pain overwhelming him. His mind flashed to the death of little Katy first, then watching as his beloved Caroline suffered with the same illness, and to that day where he saw Johnny stabbed through the chest with a sword, the darkness of his grave, and finally on the faces of the four men responsible for most of his grief.

He tossed and turned, his mind desperately trying to push back against the despair and darkness.

The fight was over.

He sat bolt upright, suddenly and surprisingly awake. He sat up from his bedroll. Dawn was rising in the east, rolling back the darkness with long, orange tendrils of light.

Chisenhall took a bite of the jerky that was in the saddlebag and popped open his canteen. He leaned back against his saddle once more, chewed the jerky, and sipped from the canteen. He watched the dark form of his staked-out and quiet steed, looking as dead as he felt – or maybe had felt. He could barely remember the man in the room, the former tobacco chewing, tobacco juice spilling, man dressed all in black. Recalled now a gaping red hole in the man's forehead, brains, bone fragments, and blood – lots of blood – spewed behind the man on the wall and the floor. He barely remembered pulling the knife from the man's hand – the knife he had pinned him to the floor with.

Had he been scorched down that deep inside himself? Had the very life of him been snatched out of him? And then the thoughts again of the sword being pushed through Johnny like a pig on a spit. Thought of himself nearly six feet under a pile of dirt, lying there not too far away from the graves of his children and his wife.

They'd made him dig one grave too many.

His world was gone. He got up, put his gear away, saddled the horse, started on this path again – a path that was leading him east. The moment of feeling that had returned was now a distant memory. A speck of dirt blown away with the wind. And he swore, he intended never to allow himself to experience those feelings again.

A stone sharpens steel.

And he was the steel.

BOOK 2

MESILLA

CHAPTER 8

A NEW COMPLICATION

Annie May Allison wavered right and left, nearly dropping off the back of the grey mare. She had lost a lot of blood, and her right leg pained her something dreadful. About half the blood felt to be in her riding boot.

The night was black as pitch, and she could not see her hand before her eyes. The rain made visibility worse, and only for brief moments when the lightning reached down from the clouds was she able to view the trail. On either side of her were trees, and more trees. She couldn't really see them – it was that awfully dark – but she knew they were standing there like giant pillars along a long fence line.

She had trekked this route many times before, and only the grey mare knew it better than she did. Tonight, it was in the grey mare that she trusted. If she could just stay in the damn saddle.

She was in so much pain she thought she might cry out at any moment, but that would not be sensible or helpful. What with the rain and the lightning, who was to hear her screams – apart from maybe those who had shot her in the leg to begin with – though she questioned if they were still about. Before she got too light-headed from blood loss, she took advantage of the familiarity she possessed of the area to lose them, and now there was the impending storm and its blanket of blackness that helped to hide her. Yes, nothing sensible or helpful in a scream or cry, nothing at all.

Annie May smiled to herself. Her father always thought she was too darn sensible, she thought. But then the intensity of the pain washed over her again, a dense, hot surge of it. Her head rolled and her eyes glazed over. It seemed awfully dreamlike that she was straddling Old Susanna out here in the darkness of night, a thunderstorm howling up and shooting out lightning all around her, a chuck of lead in her thigh.

A bolt of lightning ripped a hole in the black sky for an instant.

Annie May blinked and tried to clear the glaze before her eyes by a sheer effort of will power. Had she seen someone else on the trail? A shadow perhaps?

Pitch blackness took over again, like the deepest well she'd ever seen, a well that went on forever.

Another bolt lit up the sky.

Yeah, now she was sure she wasn't alone along the trail. A man. And not just any man – a really big man who sat high in the saddle. Annie May tried to get the small pistol out of her belt and hold the reins, but it was a hell of a struggle to do both. She hoped she didn't shoot herself in her other thigh trying to get the weapon out. But if she did, there couldn't be much blood left in her to lose, she thought – and for a strange, faint second, that made her laugh slightly.

She was wandering away into a haze of nothingness. The pistol felt exceptionally hefty, despite its small size – in fact it felt more like a large rock, difficult to grasp. . . .

It fell from her hand and into the damp earth of the trail, and then, as if in a slow-moving dream, she began to slip from the saddle. Slipping to the right, hanging on to the saddle horn. . . .

A bolt of lightning flashed.

The man tall in the saddle was closer now, riding forward at a slow, deliberate pace.

Darkness, and not just the night now reached out for her: it was in her mind, in her soul.

Her final thought as she fell from Old Susanna and hit the wet ground was that they had found her.

Chisenhall had witnessed the girl in the first flash of lightning, but at first look, dressed as she was in men's clothing and hat, he had thought she was a man.

He questioned that any law or worse were on his trail this quickly. It hadn't been that long back that he had killed the man in black in Room 4 above the saloon, and no one knew where he was headed. But still, from here on out he would be extremely careful to avoid unwanted attention – even if it seemed highly improbable that a bounty hunter or lawman might be riding directly into him on a rainy night trail.

When the lightning lit up the sky a second time, he had two of the three pistols he carried already out and ready for use, hammers cocked. But now he could see that this rider was injured, wilting in the saddle like a limp wildflower. And when they tried to draw a pistol, he was already returning his to his gunbelt, knowing full well the rider was not going to be capable of using theirs – they were scarcely steady enough to draw a breath, much less a bead on him.

Then Annie May's hat fell from her head, and her lush, reddish-brown hair tumbled free, looking very much like rich mahogany in the sudden lightning flare, which outlined it strikingly against the darkness of the night. She slipped right over and dropped unceremoniously into the mud with a thud. Her grey mare kept plodding along deliberately toward Chisenhall.

He bent down from his saddle and grabbed the grey mare's

reins. He got down from his roan, and leading both horses went over to the crumpled woman, finding her more from recollection than by sight, as it was pitch black still.

He had to wait until the next flash of lightning to see her at all, and when it came he could tell the woman was not doing well. Her face was as white as winter snow. But even in that condition, she was also noticeably pretty and remarkably young – maybe late teens or early twenties, Chisenhall guessed.

He reached down and picked her up in his arms. He immediately recognized the warm liquid on his arms that was oozing through his shirt as blood.

The girl was injured far worse than he had at first thought.

He gently lowered her down to the ground, then felt along her leg and thigh until he found the wound. He took out his knife and cut away part of her pants leg, slitting it carefully up the side clear to her waist. He was forced to wait for the lightning flashes to get a look at the leaking wound again, and this time he got an eyeful. It was extremely bad, though in the poor light it may have just looked worse than it truly was.

Chisenhall unwrapped the bandana from around his neck; then working as if he were a blind man, more by feel than sight, somehow he managed to place a handful of wet mud on the wound and tie the bandana around her leg. Then he picked her up once more and put her on his horse, holding her in place with one hand while he tried to climb up behind her. It was a struggle, but eventually he managed to do this. Then leading the grey mare, he spun the animals round and started back in the direction from which the woman had been riding.

She had obviously been trying to put wherever she was coming from behind her, but she needed immediate medical attention, and all Ross Chisenhall knew was that Mesilla was also in that direction, and nothing was keeping him from going there.

He had been sticking to the forest trails for the past few

47

days, and the last directions he had been given were from a nearby rancher in Antony. The farmer's name was Brent Mullen. If the man had been apprehensive of Chisenhall, him carrying three revolvers and having a new pink scar on his face, he didn't show it. Chisenhall had helped him out by chopping some wood, and when he left, Mullen had told him how to find Mesilla, the biggest piece of trash town between Antony and Kinlaw.

Well, he might be off his course some, and there wasn't any map to follow, but Chisenhall knew he had to get there, and get there pretty quickly, or the woman would die. She was oozing blood through his makeshift patch and soaking his own pants leg, which was pushed up tight against the back of her leg. It appeared she had been shot, and it looked to have gone clean through the leg, but if it had or it hadn't, it wouldn't matter much if she died from blood loss.

Chisenhall forced his leg up tighter against the back of the woman's wounded leg and kept working his way – albeit not as fast as he would have liked – along the timberland trail. Less than an hour later the sky began to clear some. Nothing to give thanks about, but he could see more clearly, and he was happy about that. It looked as if he was working his way out of the forest now.

If he had Mullen's bearings right, a hard ride for about another hour or so and he would have made it to Mesilla. But he doubted if the girl had another hour of life in her.

He was holding her upright with his right arm and controlling the horse with the other. Her flesh had seemed a tad tepid through the damp shirt at first, yet now her body was less warm. He wondered if she were dead already.

Now that he could see plainly, he kicked the horse faster across the clearing and up a long sloping hill – strangely high for this part of the country, and probably, Chisenhall thought, an old Indian burial mound – and from its top, though still some distance yet, he could see faint lights: the town of Mesilla.

CHAPTER 9

WHAT IF THE GIRL IS DEAD?

The foremost thing that Chisenhall thought as he arrived via Mesilla's Main Street – in fact the only street in the town – was, what if the girl is dead? And what concerned him the most about that thought was that he might be coerced to slow down his search for Rake Hanley. As to whether anyone might think that he killed the girl, he didn't care.

He had become cold.

Well, what had he decided about it taking stone to sharpen steel?

He rode down the town's only street looking right and then left. The place with the most lights appeared to be – and this did not surprise him – the town's saloon. That made complete sense. It was the one place with the most action, but in a little town like Mesilla there probably would not be much action to begin with.

That could change if he found Hanley here. But that had not happened yet.

He didn't stop at the saloon, but instead rode on past, trying to be as quiet as a church mouse so as not to create more trouble before he was ready. If he didn't find what or whom he was looking for quickly, then he would make a point of going to the saloon – and he also needed to find the girl a doctor. Fortunately he didn't have to look too long.

Not far below the saloon on the left was a big wooden building with a small house attached to the side. At the rear a light burned in the window. Out front of it hung a sign that said in white paint: MEDICAL DOCTOR. Simple enough, he thought.

Chisenhall stopped in front of the office and scrambled down off his roan; he succeeded in pulling down the woman after him with some care. She looked to be not too far from death, if not dead already. He carried her up the steps and kicked the door angrily.

It was a brief moment before a slender, baldheaded man with grey patches of hair on either side of his head, and a crooked pair of spectacles placed across the bridge of his nose, came in answer to his kick to the door.

The balding man wore an accepting look, the sort that Chisenhall had seen other sawbones develop in his past experiences, in their handling of gruesome injuries and deaths. The look faded to one of deep apprehension as soon as the doctor saw the woman in Chisenhall's arms.

'Quickly, in here,' the man commanded before Chisenhall could try to explain the situation.

Chisenhall did as he was instructed and brought her inside, and the sawbones went from lamp to lamp, lighting each.

'Go on and put her right there' – the doctor motioned to a wooden platform that stood erect in the center of the room, supported by a thick post. It didn't appear to be as comfortable as a bed, but Chisenhall did as he was told. The sawbones came quickly over to the table with one of the lamps in his hands, and set it down just about level with the girl's head. He pulled back her eyelids, then checked the pulse on her neck.

'Will she be . . . ?' Chisenhall started, then paused. '. . . I mean, is she . . . ?'

When the sawbones did not answer, Chisenhall walked back to the door and closed it. He then returned to the doctor and the woman on the table. He waited a moment before stating, 'I reckon from the way she was bleeding on me, she has a bullet in her leg there.'

'I reckon you'd be right in that assertion,' the doctor replied.

'Well, I'll be goin' now, thanks for takin' care of her.'

'Going? Most certainly you will not!' the doctor scolded him. 'I shall need some help with her. Now, there's a stove right there. Stoke it up. Get the fire nice and hot. Pour some water out of that bucket over there and into that larger bucket. I will be needing some boiling water and I need it as soon as possible. Understand?' When Chisenhall stood there in silence looking at the sawbones, the doctor snapped, 'Get moving, mister!'

Ross Chisenhall did as he was told, and when the water was on the boil, he went back to the doctor and looked down at the woman he had carried in.

'She going to make it, doc?'

'She's lost a lot of blood, you should have brought her to me sooner,' the doctor said. 'She's not looking so good.'

'I didn't . . .' Chisenhall started to argue but watched as the doctor placed a thin pillow beneath the girl's head and removed the mud and his makeshift bandanna bandage.

After a few minutes, the doctor looked up at him and said, 'This crude thing,' indicating the bandage that he had tossed on to the floor, 'just may have stopped the blood loss long enough to save her life. It's filthy as hell, but it did stop the blood loss considerably.'

'Good to hear.'

'I'm not excusing you, sir, or deeming you a doctor, mind you, but what you did helped.'

'I heard you the first time, and I don't care to be a doctor,' Chisenhall explained.

'Well then, be quiet and bring me some towels out of that chest across the room,' the sawbones pointed, 'and then use the pot hook to bring me that pot of boiling water. Set it on this stand, right here.'

Again, Chisenhall found himself doing as he was told – he got the towels from the chest, tossed them over one shoulder, hooked the boiling pot of water and carried it over to set on the stand – not the most elegant stand, but it did what it was asked to do.

When Chisenhall stood next to the doctor again he saw the sawbones had removed the woman's clothes. Despite the situation, Chisenhall could not help but notice the woman's features. She was thin, with small, round breasts, and as he looked her up and down, he felt guilty as if he had betrayed the memory of Caroline. He turned his head away sharply.

'Don't tell me you ain't seen a woman naked before, mister,' the doctor said.

'Only my wife.'

'Oh, well, good for you,' the doctor replied with admiration. 'Start dipping those towels in the water. Get them good and soaked now, use the pot hook so as not to burn yourself.'

'Learn that in doctoring school, did you?'

The sawbones surprised Chisenhall with a chuckle, and went over to the stove where he began clanging something metal about. He came back, took the soaked towels from Chisenhall and began to clean the woman's wound.

'Do you know who she is?' Chisenhall asked.

'Yeah, this is Annie May Allison. Old Jack Allison's gal. She's as tough as they come,' the sawbones replied.

'This short of thing happen a lot around Mesilla? The shooting of women, I'm askin'?'

The doctor looked at Chisenhall, seemed to let his eyes rest on the scar for the first time. 'Seems all sorts of things – good and bad – happen all over the place, mister.'

Chisenhall did not reply.

The sawbones pulled a little black bag from beneath the platform, took out a few bottles and unstopped them. He said to Chisenhall, 'Need you to check that iron I have in the fire there. Tell me if it's good and hot.'

Chisenhall walked over to the stove and looked in. 'It's red hot,' he noted.

'We're gonna see if there is any fight left in Annie May once I use that to cauterize the wound,' the doctor said.

Chisenhall winced. During the war he had seen many on-the-spot wound cauterizations with a heated knife blade or gun barrel. It was not a pleasant sight.

'Grab some of those rags from the chest where you got the towels,' the sawbones said. 'Use those to grab the iron, and bring it on over here.'

Chisenhall frowned, got the rags, and went back to grab the red-hot iron. He brought it to the sawbones, white smoke floating off it in a slothful manner.

Carefully, the doctor took the rags and the iron from Chisenhall. 'Now, get on her other side and hold her down. I'm gonna hold her on this side and put this to her wound. Now you have to be ready and hold her tight. It won't be easy, now.'

'The bullet looks as if it went clean through the leg,' Chisenhall noted. 'I mean, I think it did, right?'

'Who's the doctor here? Get over there and hold her down. This red-hot iron could bring a man – or woman – back from the dead once I lay it to the wound.'

Chisenhall slid around to the other side of the platform, took hold of the woman just about the knee, reached out and put his weight on her shoulder.

'Ready?' the doctor asked.

'I reckon I am.'

'You reckon, or are you sure?'

'I'm ready, come on with it,' Chisenhall fired back.

'OK, I'm goin' to put it to her.'

And the doctor did just that. Silver smoke wafted up from the woman's flesh. The odor of the scorching flesh was sickening. Chisenhall held the woman down with all his strength. He watched her face, and when the iron touched her skin, she was alive in a second. Her body pitched, but he was able to hold her down. Her eyes jolted open, and he saw them look at him in amazement, but not with acknowledgement. She was still behind the haze of agony and blood loss. But in that moment, for she abruptly closed her eyes and flopped back on to the platform in a faint, he had looked into the sable blue eyes and felt a bizarre stinging of something he thought had been buried back in the grave he'd dug himself out of.

CHAPTER 10

HEALING IS A MATTER OF TIME

There was concern on Ross Chisenhall's face. 'You reckon the girl is gonna live, doc?'

'If I were a betting man,' the doctor started, 'and I am not . . . I would bet she will. Now, you aren't lookin' so good yourself, mister.'

Chisenhall managed a grin.

'That scar might heal up fine,' the doctor noted, ' . . . in time.' The sawbones then motioned to the girl.

Chisenhall understood. 'What, to do the other side, where the bullet exited, huh?'

'Yes. We have got to. Where the bullet comes out is always more damaged.'

The iron went back into the fire and they repeated the procedure of cauterizing the wound, the only difference being that this time Annie May did not move at all.

'She's not moving at all, Doc. Is that good or bad?'

'Hard to tell at this point. The body works in mysterious ways, my friend. It can only take a certain amount of pain before it knocks us out. Now, we are done. If you could lay her on the bed, I would greatly appreciate that, or rather, my old back would. Make sure she is covered up nice and completely. Can't have you gawking over her naked flesh now, can we?'

Chisenhall was not amused.

'Come on with it, she needs her rest.'

Kindly, Chisenhall picked her up from the wooden platform and went where the doctor had motioned the bed was, in a small warm room off the back. 'This room is for patients only. I may be able to scramble up enough to add another visitor's room later this year. This town is on the verge of expanding. And if I'm still here, I would like to have more room.'

Chisenhall placed Annie May in the bed and followed this by pulling the blankets around the poor woman's naked and badly wounded body.

'Let her rest now, I will check on her in a little while. You up for some coffee? You done wrecked my night, might as well enjoy a cup of coffee with me.'

'Sure . . . reckon coffee sounds good.'

'Don't make it sound like a chore, geez. C'mon. . . .'

'I didn't mean to. . . .' Chisenhall started when the doctor smiled at him.

'Oh, don't go gettin' all offended, I was just joshin' with ya.'

Chisenhall returned the man's smile, understanding that it was the first time he had felt anything other than hatred in days. But he couldn't allow himself to get too soft now, he wasn't finished: he had to find Hanley.

The two men went back to the main room and the doctor wasted little time in brewing a pot of coffee and pouring each of them a cup. The room was a bit stuffy and warm. The old sawbones went to the window and opened it a tad.

'I never got your name, Doc. Sorry, plumb forgot to ask,' Chisenhall noted.

'That's OK, I didn't get yours, either,' the doctor said. 'Mine's Sam Griffith.'

Chisenhall hesitated. There would soon be lawmen looking

for Ross Chisenhall he figured. 'John Hall.'

'You say that unpleasantly,' Doc Griffith said. 'Like it's not your real name, but you wanted to make sure I thought that it was.'

'Listen. . . .'

'Aw, quiet now. I don't care who you are or what your name is. You look straight enough to me. You brought Annie May in, didn't you?'

'And you are certain that I didn't do that to her?'

'That would make sense, wouldn't it? You shot her down, then go out of your way to bring her to me, then help me hold her down as I apply a hot iron to her. And the way you looked at her naked flesh . . . well, not someone who'd shot a woman and appreciated their finer points too.'

Chisenhall shook his head. 'You probably get hit a lot, don't you, Doc?'

'Not at all. I'm old enough that people hate me, or hate to hurt me, whatever you want to believe. I've earned the right to be a tad odd, and you will too, if you make it to my age. I like to bicker, argue and read. How about you?'

'I don't read . . . much,' Chisenhall said taking a seat in a nearby chair. 'I mean, I never learned to read. . . .'

'That's a tragedy, sorry. You ought to learn how. The world opens to a man who can read. Want me to take a look at that scar of yours?'

Chisenhall reached up and touched the raw wound. 'Mishap.'

'I bet.'

Doc Griffith went over to the stove and checked on the coffee, went in the back and brought out two ceramic cups and poured them up a cup each of the brew. He handed Chisenhall his and seated himself on the platform where Annie May had just lay. There was blood on it, but it didn't seem to bother the old sawbones.

'You know,' the doc said, 'I reckon that maybe I could do

something for that scar. It doesn't seem to be that old. I would guess you haven't had it longer than a week or more.'

'Nah, that's all right. I think I've seen all the doctorin' I want to see in my lifetime.'

Doc Griffith chuckled, sipped his coffee, set it on the platform, and slipped off. 'Nonsense, I'll take a look.'

Chisenhall went to protest. 'It's all right, I said. I'm OK.'

'You may be, but that scar isn't. It looks infected. Want to lose your life?'

Chisenhall didn't say anything, but neither did he resist when the old sawbones bent to examine the scar.

'Mostly scabbed over,' the doc said. 'That's a good sign, believe it or not, and some of it is ready to come off. But you got some pus pockets, and I was right, it is infected.'

Chisenhall sighed heavily. 'You are a persistent son-of-a-gun, aren't you?'

'For sure.'

Chisenhall gave in. 'All right. Fine. Get on with it.'

The older man went over to his black bag, opened it and returned to Chisenhall. He bent over him, eyeing the wound and asked, 'I'd say . . . best guess . . . knife wound.'

'Close.'

'This have anything to do with your being in this part of the country, what was the name you gave me . . . John Hall?'

'Am I not allowed to travel or go where I want in this country?'

'Sure. I meant no offense. Just we don't see many visitors or travelers in these parts. So, I guessed that you were here for some reason. Perhaps it has to do with this fresh wound and nasty scar. That is what I would hazard to guess, anyway.'

'Hazard to guess, huh? You think you know everything?'

The old doctor shook his head. 'I know I don't know everything, my boy.'

Chisenhall cried out in pain as Griffith pulled some of the scab off.

'Oh, stop your whining ... just some of the dried scab being removed ... geez. Who are you here looking for, Mr Hall?'

'Who said I was looking for anyone?'

'Fine. I'll leave you alone. Have it your way.'

The doctor stripped off some more scab, and with a small needle opened the discharge pockets and cleansed them out with alcohol, hoping to stave off the infection. 'Any better?' he asked when he finished.

'How the hell should I know? You're the sawbones,' Chisenhall fired back.

'That scar ain't gonna be so bad now, I reckon. Left alone and it would have wrinkled up might nasty.'

'Helps me remember,' muttered Chisenhall.

'Well, maybe once it heals up you can forget.'

'I never will forget. Should have let it fester ... just like. . . .'

'Well, too late now. Perhaps it's best to move on. As Hippocrates said, "Healing is a matter of time, but it is sometimes also a matter of opportunity".'

'My time is up. I've already made up my mind on what I'm doing. I can't stop it now.'

'Really? That so? Umm ... if you say so. I was right, though, you did come here looking for someone.'

'I didn't say that I was looking for anyone.'

'Pretty much did, my boy.' The old man went back to the platform, sat down again, and sipped his now tepid coffee. 'If I was a bettin' man, I say it's got to do with a man named Hanley.'

Chisenhall moistened his lips with his tongue. 'You think so?'

'I do. Hanley is the worst person we have in this town – the only people that may be worse than him are the scum that work for him.'

'Work for him?'

The look on the old man's face was of shock. 'Don't tell me

you want to work for him?'

'Not at all.' Chisenhall stood and paced a few seconds. 'All right. I'm looking for Rake Hanley. But how did you guess?'

The doc's face suddenly went forbidding and firm. 'This town ain't much. One street of flimsy shacks and one sorry saloon, but it wasn't too bad a place to live before Hanley came to town. He came here just over a year or so ago, bought the saloon. I believe it is time for him to leave our town. He is always up to no good, I'm certain about that. He has money, and property around the area. I reckon he's into robbing the good folk. Lot of . . . umm . . . less than nice characters drift in and out of town with him, too.

'Couple o' days back he came back into town, and the very next thing I hear is that old Ted Wallace was selling out. He loved his land, worked hard to make something of it. He wouldn't have just up and sold it unless he was threatened or something. That girl you brought to me, the one asleep in my back room, Annie May, she and her old man Jack, those two are one tough pair. He's got a few hands and a decent-sized ranch outside of town . . . a fair ride from here, about four miles on the other side of them hills.'

'Must have been where she was goin' when I found her,' Chisenhall noted.

'Could have been, yeah, that makes sense,' Griffith said. 'But I do know one thing, which is that that no-account polecat Hanley and his lackies want to run the Allisons off their land. But they don't run too easy, even if they are outnumbered or outgunned. I think they hit Annie May here as some kind of warning. But they'll get more violent if they don't get what they want.'

'Think Annie May's old man will sell?'

'That is one stubborn man. Hard to say. But I'm afraid of what tonight's action will make him do.' He nodded toward the bedroom where Annie May slept. 'How would you take it if your woman was shot up?'

Chisenhall was hushed, a cheerless outline seemed to skulk across his face.

'Or is that why you're here?'

Chisenhall didn't answer the old man directly. 'Tell me something. If I were looking for Hanley, where might I go looking for him?'

'Now, before I tell you that, I reckon I ought to warn you. He has a tight hold on this town, and he has many men to help him keep his grip over it.'

'OK.'

'OK, and you're going to kill any of these fellas who get in your way?'

'I might.'

'And you can do this all by your lonesome, huh?'

Chisenhall eyed the doctor. 'I just want Hanley.'

'Well, he is the head of the snake and bad enough. But I figure he will want his men to protect him.'

'Any of those men have a bad eye, a young kid, in all honesty?'

The doctor gave a measured reply: 'Every once in a while I seen him with a fella that fits that description, but I haven't seen him of late.'

'Said they split up.'

'What? Who?'

'It's nothing, just thinkin' about something someone told me. About Hanley and these others splitting up.'

'Really? I'd like to hear about that conversation.'

Chisenhall smirked. 'You're a nosy old fart, aren't you?'

'I can't deny that. What the hell else I got to do, 'sides reading books, patching people up and listening to gossip?'

Chisenhall wasn't sure why, but he felt he could trust the doctor. So he told him what happened . . . all of it.

'Can't say that I blame you,' the doctor replied. 'Still, what you did to that guy in the brothel was pretty. . . .'

'Nasty?'

'I was thinkin' more towards an eye for an eye. Let's just say, for the sake of argument, you were going a little too far with it.'

'Perhaps.'

'I ain't tryin' to tell you what to do. If I were in your shoes, I wouldn't let anyone tell me what to do, either. You'll have your hands full, here in Mesilla. I'm a bit too old and too scared to help you, too. Besides, town's got to have a doctor, and wouldn't do me no good to get myself killed, as sounds like my skills are going to be needed. And on account that you look plumb silly with them old revolvers stickin' out of your belt there, and just one holstered, I'm gonna give you somethin'.'

The doctor walked over to a cabinet and opened it. He pulled out a holstered revolver and undid the ammo belt from around it. He pulled out the revolver and handed it to Chisenhall.

'What you have in your hand is a Colt cartridge revolver. A man was just passing through town and paid me with that. Colt started making this type a few years back. The ammo belt has some cartridges in it, and here is a box of some more.'

Ross Chisenhall stood up, unbuckled his gun, and strapped on the one the doctor handed him.

'Those cartridges are a hell of a lot neater and easier to use,' Doc Griffith said.

'I never had the money to buy a gun like this before. I've seen them, though.'

'You own one now. Though it might be hard to find more cartridges around here, at least for a few more years, I reckon. I do have a lefty holster, too, if you want to use it for that other pistol on your left.'

Chisenhall's look answered, without him saying a word.

Doc Griffith produced a holster from the bottom cabinet, took the old revolver out of it, and handed it to Chisenhall.

Chisenhall strapped it on and slipped his own pistol into it.

'I guess you'll still go out with the other two sticking out of your pants, then?'

Chisenhall removed the other two revolvers in the process of strapping on the holsters, but now carefully picked them up to inspect each before pushing then into his gun belt. 'Sometimes I reckon I will. If you want my old holster, it's yours, Doc. One more thing, Doc?'

'Shoot,' the old man smiled as he said that. Chisenhall gave a slight smile in return.

'I was just figuring that the left-handed holster was yours, if I'm correct. Am I?'

The doctor shrugged.

'I noticed you worked left-handed most of the time when you were fixin' up Annie May in there,' Chisenhall continued.

'Pretty observant fella, aren't you?' The doctor grinned at him and turned to the room where Annie May slept. He went in and closed the door behind him.

Chisenhall helped himself to another cup of coffee, and after a few moments, the old sawbones returned from the back room.

'She doin' OK?'

'Fair enough. She's a tough lady, she'll pull through.'

Chisenhall nodded. 'That's good.'

'I was plannin' on riding out to the Allison place first light and tell Jack his little girl was all right. Bet he's worried somethin' fierce right about now. No, better yet, I should ride out there right this instant so that he doesn't do somethin' foolish like ride into town and get himself shot up over there at Hanley's saloon. And I tell you, Mr Hall, I know you got revenge and killing on your mind, and that you're ready to go about your business, but if I were you, I would use that head of yours and rein in that hate. Wait for a better time, and then nail the polecat Hanley.'

Chisenhall smiled. 'That makes a heap of sense, Doc. I'm feelin' a tad sensible right at this moment.'

'Good to hear, my boy. You lock this door behind me and toss out there in my bed if you like. By the looks of you, a few hours o' sleep would do you good.' The doctor turned and then added, 'Doctor's orders.'

Doc Griffith picked up his hat and pushed it on his head. 'People don't pay too much attention to my comings and goings. One of the perks of being a doctor. I can come and go as I please.' He opened the door. 'Remember, lock this door behind me, you hear me?'

CHAPTER 11

DREAMS, REVOLVERS AND ALLIES

That night Ross Chisenhall dreamt again, this time more intensely than on the trail. His marriage to Caroline. The births of his children, the war, and then that day by the graveside. Not going back now, but advancing in order.

And then he was in shadows and his breath was brisk. It seemed everything was pressing on him, getting closer and closer. He grasped quickly that he was in the grave below ground with six feet of dirt on top of him.

Abruptly revolvers were in his hands, for he had slept with them by his sides, and he sat bolt upright in bed with the revolvers pointed before him at the door of – where was he? Slowly he realized where it was he had woken up: in the doctor's room in a town called Mesilla. Somewhere in this town, or on the fringes, was the man he was here to find. And when that business was concluded there were others.

He swung his feet off the bed and stared at the room. Light was peeking through the curtains, and he could see well enough. The cabinets, the row of books – the home of a soft, non-violent man with no vengeance to hand out. Somehow he coveted this way of life. Perhaps it was because his life had been so noiseless and non-violent once before – and not that long ago. And then there had been Caroline.

And thinking of her brought his mind to Annie May. The attractive, rough woman in the other room. The thought of her was agreeable. He swung himself back on the bed and stretched out, putting the revolvers on either side of him. He would have to be damn cautious he did not shoot the doctor when he returned to his own house.

The old man was right: he had to channel some of that hate, or become as evil as the men who made him feel this way. The doctor hadn't said that the night before, but that's what he had meant, just not in those words.

Chisenhall thought of the man he had nailed to the floor with a knife, the man he had cold-bloodedly killed. The thought made him ill.

But having to do it all over again, he would have done nothing different.

It took some time, but sleep came to him, just not as deeply as before.

Chisenhall awoke to the jangle of wheels. He had slept perhaps another hour at the most, but surely no more than that. It was now squarely day.

He rolled out of bed, fastened on the holsters, and put the revolvers in their place. He liked the feel of the new Colt Doc Griffith had given him. It was lighter, and balanced well for the hand. He put the other two pistols in his belt, pulled the covers back on the bed, and slipped on his boots.

Hearing a key turn in the lock, he went out of the bedroom and into the front room, the room that held the platform and the big cast-iron stove.

Doc Griffith came in, and behind him a thick, short man

with storm-cloud gray hair and eyes to match entered the room. He had his hat in his left hand. He wore rough clothes and his face looked well worn, like dried leather. Chisenhall knew instantly that he was a rancher, and of course that he was Annie May's father, Jack Allison.

Allison looked at Chisenhall, took in the hard, dark eyes, the pistols on either hip and those sticking out of his belt. Like Doc Griffith, he knew this was a man that meant business, and he knew, too, that there was much distress in the man's face. He was no outsider to distress himself.

He walked straight over to Chisenhall and held out his hand.

'Jack Allison,' he said. 'I want to thank you for bringing my girl in here to see Doc Griffith.'

Chisenhall shook the man's hard, firm hand. 'John . . .' the name he had given Doc Griffith the night before nearly escaped his memory, and he was scrabbling to recall it when the doctor interrupted:

'This is John Hall, Jack.'

There was a brief exchange of looks between Chisenhall and the doctor, though it went unnoticed by Allison.

Jack Allison then said, 'You saved my Annie May's life. Much obliged to you.'

'The doc did all the real work. He's the one that saved her life,' replied Chisenhall.

'He told me that if not for what you had done to her wound on the trail, Annie May might've bled to death.'

Chisenhall grinned sparsely, a bit taken aback by the sudden flood of admiration. 'Just glad I was there to help.'

'I am in your debt, son.'

'Not at all.'

Allison turned to Griffith. 'I would like to see Annie May, if I could?'

'Of course,' Doc Griffith said. 'Where is my head? I will let you wake her up. She's in there.' He nodded toward the bedroom where Annie May slept.

'Thank you,' Jack Allison said, and he went in and closed the door behind him gently.

'Want some coffee?' the doc asked.

'Sure. Sounds great,' Chisenhall replied.

'I'll fix enough for all of us, and some breakfast too. Doesn't that sound wonderful? Hope that girl can get some food in her, sure would help the healing process.'

'I know I could eat,' announced Chisenhall.

Doc Griffith went about the task of clattering pans and boiling water.

Not long after Jack Allison came out of the bedroom bearing a smile on his face. He closed the door behind him.

'She dozed off again, I'm afraid,' he said. 'One tough girl, my Annie May.'

'She tell you what happened to her?' Chisenhall asked.

Allison's face twisted. 'Yes. Said she got attacked in the dark by unknown men on her way back home. I sent her out yesterday for some supplies and ammunition. Unfortunately, ammunition is somethin' we all need a lot of, what with those night riders. That's who got her, I'm sure of it – Rake Hanley and his goons.' Jack Allison's face suddenly broke into a smile. 'She told me she thinks she hit one of the raiders, in the chest or so.'

'Are there a lot of these raiders?' Chisenhall asked.

'Enough of them to be a problem. Five, maybe six, she wasn't sure. That darn horse of hers gave her quite the run.'

Chisenhall nodded. 'I brought the horse in too, just so you know.'

'Thank you. I saw that. Much obliged. Where is Doc Griffith?'

'Making some food, I reckon.'

'I want to thank you both for saving my girl,' Jack Allison said.

Chisenhall waved off the man. 'I've been thanked plenty,

not necessary.'

'Well, I can't thank you and the doc enough.' The man paused then. He had a pained look on his face. 'Doc mentioned that you may have a beef with Hanley. Now . . . he didn't say what that beef was, and I ain't aiming to pry. He only told me on account that he likes you and wants me to hire you on.'

'Hire me? I didn't come to Mesilla lookin' for no job,' Chisenhall replied.

'Don't get your dander up, Mr Hall.' It was Doc Griffith, and he held a frying pan in his right hand, a thick potholder wrapped around its handle, and a bunch of eggs in it ready for the stove. He put it on the stove, and while he stoked up the fire he added, 'I think you ought to listen to Mr Allison here about hiring you on. I think you do want a job.'

'You do, huh? Why?'

'You got business with Hanley, right?'

Chisenhall nodded. 'And I didn't really want that information to be spread around town.'

'C'mon, there ain't no better man in Mesilla than Jack Allison. You and he are cut from the same cloth, as far as I can tell. He doesn't hold any love for Rake Hanley, and not just because of that pretty young girl in the back room, either.'

'His land, I reckon,' Chisenhall noted.

'That is one reason for sure, but there are others, too,' Doc Griffith said.

'The doc is right,' Allison said. 'Neither of us means to meddle in the affairs of another man, and I don't mean to force your hand, as anyone who opposes Hanley is likely to meet with violence. I plan on going against him with you or without. I gotta stop him from takin' my land and hurting those I love. I got some men on my side, but not a one of 'em are gunmen. They're farmers, ranchers and the like.'

'I, too, am a farmer . . . or was, up until a week ago. Why do you think I'll be any different from the rest of your men?'

'The answer is simple, Mr Hall,' Allison said. 'You are

invested in this business with Hanley for the same reason I am
– personally. It is my ranch and land that Hanley wants to take
from me, by any means necessary, apparently. I won't dance
around any longer, I'll be direct with you, Mr Hall: throw in
with me, and together we can stand against Hanley and his
raiders. What do you say?'

Chisenhall deliberated quietly for a moment. 'I don't know,
Mr Allison. . . .'

That was enough to set off Doc Griffith. 'Now wait a darn
minute here, John,' the old man said. 'You don't want that low-
down, no-account Hanley to get away with all that he has done,
do ya?'

'It's not that simple,' said Chisenhall.

'Then throw in with Jack here and be smart about things.
There is strength in numbers. Right now, Hanley has the
greater numbers, and it only makes sense to join in with others
who want the same as you. Does it matter if your vengeance
comes at your hands alone, or that it comes?'

'That all sounds fine and dandy, Doc,' Chisenhall said. 'But
I have to be the one who kills Hanley.'

'That works for me,' Allison said, 'as long as it doesn't make
sense for me or someone else to do so in the order of things.
Like if I return fire and hit him, things just happen in a fire
fight and a man can't always control them. Otherwise, Hanley
is yours to do with what you want.'

Chisenhall rubbed his chin as he considered some more.
'Mr Allison, you got yourself a deal.'

'Sounds good,' Allison said.

'Ah, damn, my eggs are burnin'!' The old man went over to
the stove and jerked the frying pan off the fire. 'Hell's bells,
might want to just start over.'

'Keeping the doc busy will also keep him quiet,' noted
Chisenhall.

'I doubt there is anything in this world that can keep that man
quiet,' Allison added, and the two men smiled at each other.

CHAPTER 12

A NEW HOME

The rain had given things a crisp, polished look – even the pines looked freshly waxed. Pools of water in the old, dirt trail shimmered rainbows in the bright morning sunlight. Ross Chisenhall sat in the back of the buckboard, cradling Annie May's sleeping head in his lap. Jack Allison drove. Their horses were tied to the back, trotting easily to the wagon's roll.

'It ain't too bumpy on her, is it?' Allison called back over his shoulder.

'Maybe if we were goin' any faster than we are now, but I reckon it's OK at this pace,' Chisenhall replied.

'I'll keep it steady, then.'

After that they rode in near silence. Chisenhall watched the countryside and took in the air. It reminded him of those crisp winter days when he went to chop firewood back home. The kids would 'help' him by chasing each other as he split the wood.

Always the memories had to lead back home – to the farm – to his family.

Chisenhall looked down at the woman and smiled. Her hair, still slightly streaked with mud and blood, was long and wild about her face. He was struck at how much she reminded him of Caroline – but not just that. She didn't actually resemble his wife all that much, there was just something about her that reminded him of her. She was younger and slightly shorter than Caroline. And despite his love of his wife's eyes, he had to admit that Annie May's eyes were the most beautiful he'd ever seen.

Somehow the stirring of feelings bothered him. He felt as if he were disrespecting Caroline for having these emotions. Why hadn't that part of him stayed buried?

When they arrived at the Allison ranch, Chisenhall was surprised to see that the log house was surrounded by a low, but solidly built barricade comprised of stones and wood. The barn had been built in a similar fashion, and about ten men stood there with rifles and pistols.

'This looks to be a big spread you got here, Mr Allison,' Chisenhall noted. 'How do you get things done?'

'It ain't easy,' Allison said proudly. 'I got a few more hands working the fields. Don't you worry, they carry guns, too. Have to in these parts. My crops can be regrown, if Hanley aims to strike at me by burning them, but my house . . . well, I would hate to have to rebuild that. Annie May was born in there. My wife died in there. I may not get much done around here, but at least we should be safe. If trouble comes, we'll be ready...' Allison reached down and produced a shotgun from under the buckboard's seat ' . . . and so will I.'

They clattered on up the well-rutted drive toward the stone and wood barn. When they had pulled up before the structure, Allison got out to throw open the wide log doors, and Chisenhall lifted up Annie May.

'I'll take her up to the house, if that's OK?' Chisenhall asked.

'Much obliged,' Allison responded. 'Just kick in the door, Slate will see that you get in all right.'

Chisenhall carried Annie May toward the home. A couple of men with rifles gathered at his side.

'What happened to Annie May?' a blond-haired younger man asked.

'Mr Allison thinks it was Hanley's raiders.'

'Those sonobitches!' the young blond man snapped.

'That'd be a safe guess,' the other man said. He was a little taller, and a lot heavier, with fingers missing from his right hand.

'Allison hire you on as a new hand?' the younger man asked.

Chisenhall nodded, then said uneasily, 'Name's John Hall.'

'I knew some Halls once, up around St Louie. You any kin to them?' the heavier man queried.

'Not that I'm aware of,' Chisenhall answered back.

They reached the house, and the portly man beat his hand on the door furiously. 'C'mon, Slate, open up. Get your ass movin'!'

Slate Cartwright was a red-haired man with a vast beard and mustache. He stood several inches or more over six feet and wasn't wearing boots when he opened the door. There was a Navy Colt revolver strapped to his hip.

'What happened to Annie May?' Slate said, standing aside so Chisenhall could carry the unconscious Annie May inside.

'Where shall I put her?' Chisenhall asked.

'In there,' Slate said pointing. 'What happened to her? And who the hell are you?"

Chisenhall was too busy carrying Annie May to answer the big man. He carried her into the room specified by Slate and stretched her out on the bed.

The youthful blond-haired man replied to Slate's questions. 'Hanley's raiders. Don't appear to be too bad, I reckon. That right, fella?'

'I suppose so.'

Chisenhall looked down then and saw that Annie May had opened her eyes. No one else seemed to be in the room but he and Annie May.

She looked at him, searching his face for some familiarity

73

with her eyes. She touched her leg, felt the strange bandaging and clothes that Doc Griffith had provided her with. She wriggled her feet as they were a tad cold as she had no socks or shoes on.

Chisenhall, as if commanded by the wriggling, gently folded a corner of the blanket over them.

'I know you,' Annie May said. 'You were there when I fell from my horse.'

'Yes, I was,' Chisenhall said. His mouth was a little dry.

'Well . . . um . . . thank you.'

'My pleasure, miss.'

'Annie May Allison,' she smiled.

'I know.'

She was still tired and weak, and was blinking slowly as she looked at him. And then she was asleep again.

Silently Chisenhall left the room and went out into the living room to meet the others and Jack Allison. But not before pulling the blanket over Annie May, just as he had for little Katy and Johnny not that long ago.

Jack Allison introduced Chisenhall to the hands, all of whom were present now. Everyone seemed to welcome him with enthusiasm. Which made sense, since Chisenhall learned that Hanley's raiders sometimes numbered close to twenty to thirty men at various times.

He also learned that there was no sheriff or law in Mesilla, and hadn't been for several months. Not since Hanley's rowdies gunned down the last sheriff, and no one else had the nerve to pick up the tin star. Allison had considered it himself, but the duties of a sheriff would have taken him away from his duties as a farmer. As for the other men – well, truth be known, they didn't like the idea of having to face off with Rake Hanley and his ruffians by day and then fight them again at night as raiders.

Allison took Chisenhall for a ride around his spread, careful not to stray too far lest some sharpshooter was hiding in the pines, or in case of any other threat around the place. Chisenhall granted the man his paranoia with due reason. He showed Chisenhall his cattle and late crops – turnips, peas, carrots and winter squash. Most of the latter had been harvested, though some had fought their last battle against Old Man Winter and had turned brown in defeat.

'Not all that much growin' at this time of the year, as you can see,' Allison said as they rode. 'But I do my best, and I'm proud of what I have. I carry my harvest into Texas, as well as Mesilla. Got buyers that come here for my crops, too. Not makin' big money, just somethin' to keep things goin'. Ain't nothing like growin' things, you know what I mean.'

'I do,' Chisenhall said, resigned.

Allison turned to him and reined up his horse. Chisenhall stopped and leaned forward in the saddle.

'You seem to have some knowledge of farming,' noted Allison.

'Yes.'

'You mentioned . . . I believe you were a farmer until about . . . ?'

'About a week or so ago.'

Allison removed his hat and scratched his head. 'Funny, you don't look or act like a farmer.'

'Should have seen me a week or so ago, I did then.'

'Well, now I would guess you look more like – a gunman, Mr Hall. But I mean no offense,' Allison offered.

'It's all right, no offense taken. Life has a way of altering a man's path. Changing him, I reckon.'

'Sorry for that. Whatever it was that happened, I'm sorry.'

Chisenhall nodded at the farmer and the two resumed riding.

After a while, Chisenhall spoke. 'What you have here, it is most certainly worth fighting for, Mr Allison.'

They broke away from the edge of the fields and into a wide

expanse of charred pine trees.

'Was a bolt of lightning that started the fire about ... I reckon almost a year ago. Been tryin' to clear the area out for more acres of farmland since.'

Chisenhall muttered a response, then after looking around added, 'I wouldn't be in a rush to clear it out, there's enough pines that aren't too burnt, and those are green 'nuff.'

'I reckon they are. They're so pretty it's hard to lumber them. I made a cabin for myself out of some. If that burns down, I'll just build another, I reckon.'

'All this Hanley's raiders business, got to be hard on your daughter, Mr Allison, right?'

Allison nodded. 'It is. But that girl is one of the tough ones, just like her mother, God rest her soul.'

'Aye, she seems to be mighty tough all right.'

Allison smiled. 'Come, John, let's ride back.'

BOOK THREE

HANLEY'S NIGHT RIDERS

CHAPTER 13

I HATE KILLIN'
HORSES

That night Hanley's Night Riders rode. The moon was in the shape of a jagged scar, long and lean and pale as bone.

They came out of the pines along midnight, about six acres down from Allison's log cabin he had built from the lightning-burned pines. They rode direct across the winter fields, fields full of peas and winter squash. Much of the squash had lost the fight against winter's bitter touch, but the peas matched the never-changing pines. Nonetheless the riders rode unfeeling for their jade beauty. On out across the field they went, crushing the crops in their path.

Twenty-one riders this night rode in pitch black sheets with masks made from burlap sacks, hellbent on creating fear and causing destruction.

He thought it was his eyes in the beginning. A large black groundswell seemed to roll out of the pines and plunge forward. And then there was the sound of hoofs, distant and thundering, growing in greatness, rising to what sounded like war drums.

'Night Riders a-comin'!' Slate shouted.

They had kept five guards on the alert, one atop the house,

one atop the barn, and the rest at the barn, which was making do as a makeshift bunkhouse.

'Night Riders a-comin'!' Slate shouted again. The word passed to the barn patrol who shouted it too.

'Hanley's riders approaching!'

Chisenhall was the first out of bed, rolling from his bunk and into his boots with swift accuracy. He came out of the barn and into the bright moonlight, a revolver in each hand, two more stuck in his belt. The other men hurried to fall in behind him.

Hanley's night riders came on with the sound of booming thunder. Rifles split the night, and up on the house, Slate Cartwright pitched back with a shriek and fell to the ground.

The raiders had come with murder as their intention.

Little patches of red bloomed in the night as the masked riders fired into the barn and house, dropping another man amongst those who defended Allison's place.

The rest of the defenders returned fire from their vantage points. Allison came out of the house with a rifle in his right hand, a shotgun in the other.

Hanley's masked riders were bearing down on the house and the barricade built to protect it.

Chisenhall dived behind some latticework of wood and stone, raising his revolver as a masked rider rode into his range, kicking up his horse, riding hard for the barricade, ready to jump from the creature.

The Colt in Chisenhall's right hand spoke to the night with a loud bang. The masked rider abruptly erupted with a jet of red from his black cloak or coat, and lurched back from his horse head over heels into the ground. The horse kept coming, jumped over the barricade, and just kept on going.

Now the masked raiders were closing, bearing down on the barricade like a swarm of locust.

Allison threw himself down beside Chisenhall.

Rifle and revolver barked and spat fire in the night. Another of Allison's men bucked forward on to his face – or what was left of it – Chisenhall turned his head away slightly at the sight of the wound. The man had taken a rifle discharge at very close range.

'They're out for blood this time,' Allison howled, and he rapidly raised up the shotgun, letting both barrels fly. The roar was followed by a tumbling of rider and horse, neither of which got up. 'I hate killin' horses,' Allison snapped.

The masked riders began to circle the barricade, each firing pointlessly and somewhat madly, trying to shoot across the barricade and into those hiding on the other side of it.

'If we survive this night I'll help you build this barricade higher,' promised Chisenhall.

A chunk of rock flew up next to his face, just whistling by him, as he spoke.

That was close, he thought.

'I hear that,' Allison replied, and he glanced up over the barricade with his rifle, firing it blindly into the throng of riders. 'But I think we're done for, they got us pinned down, outgunned and outnumbered. It is only a matter of time now.'

'I ain't givin' up just yet,' Chisenhall said. Unexpectedly he was up and running for one of the stray horses whose riders had been shot or bucked off, that were bolting around looking for some escape from the noise.

'What are you doin'?' Jack Allison called out.

'Probably something I'll regret and get me killed', Chisenhall shouted back, but Allison was out of his range to actually hear him. Chisenhall swung up on a horse and reined it until he was able to turn it in the direction he wanted to go: that was straight for the low wall, and the horse jumped.

Chisenhall's dad had told him stories of the War Between the States, when outgunned and outnumbered was common-place, and he had learned from those stories that often harshness and audacity were better weapons than rifles, guns and cannons. Or to be more precise, they at least gave the out-gunned and outnumbered side a chance.

Now he put the reins between his teeth. A revolver in each hand, shouting wildly between clenched teeth, he rode into the midst of the masked raiders, his guns spitting fire and bullets savagely.

Like a man possessed he rode, and when his revolvers spoke, men fell in reply. Four shots he pumped into one man alone, driving him back from his horse and hitting him right between the eyes with one shot, while the other three hit him in the chest before he hit the ground.

Boom! Boom! Boom!

Another masked rider was knocked off his horse, his black robe catching fire as the shot was point blank from Chisenhall.

Boom! Boom! Boom!

'Jesus, Mary and Joseph!' Allison exclaimed. 'He's actually routing them!'

Chisenhall rode down another masked rider, and this fella, perhaps in an act of bravery, perhaps just stupidity, rode to meet him. The masked rider snapped off a few shots, neither of which were well aimed and so missed their target. As for Chisenhall's revolvers, they were empty.

He dropped his pistols into the holsters, and quick as a hiccup, cross drew those revolvers in his belt, firing simultaneously at the rider who was now right on top of him.

The shots were just before the masked raider could fire again. The man's gun arm went up, but his shot was pulled high and wild as the two blasts from Chisenhall's revolvers knocked him from the saddle as if yanked by some invisible rope and lasso.

Chisenhall's momentum carried him past the fallen rider.

The injured masked raider was up and trying to run with a stumbling gait.

Chisenhall turned the horse after tucking one of the guns back into his belt and using his other hand to control the horse. He rode up behind him and shot him squarely in the back of the head in a crimson explosion.

Now the other masked riders were congregating on Chisenhall, but the remaining defenders had jumped the barricade and were approaching, their guns barking.

The attacking masked riders quickly reined in their horses, and seeing that the tide had turned, retreated and rode off to the echoes of gunfire.

CHAPTER 14

SMALL BATTLES

When the sound of gunfire had died and the chatter of the men, most of it directed at Chisenhall's heroic efforts, had subsided, they went about uncovering the masks of the dead night riders.

Chisenhall, in his gunning fury, had at first hoped Rake Hanley had been among those he had dropped in the skirmish, but as they peeled back the mask, he began to fear that he would be among the dead, and worse yet, that it had not been his bullet that had dropped him. No – he didn't want Hanley that way. He wanted to look the bastard in the eye. Man to man. See what he was made of. See him die with the lead from his revolver in his face or chest. Chisenhall's lead. Lead marked for revenge. And before Hanley died, he wanted the man to remember him, what he had done to his family, and to be aware that Chisenhall had come back from the dead himself for his ultimate vengeance.

He wondered, too, if the man with the roving eye was among the fallen. If he had parted Hanley's company for eternity.

But he was not among the bodies, and neither was Rake Hanley.

'Do you think Hanley led these men here tonight?'

Chisenhall asked Allison as the farmer ripped the hood from one of the riders.

'Not sure. Doubtful. Probably more talk than action. No sheriff around here, so it also would not surprise me if he had. Not that he needed to. Hanley's fairly wily. He might have ridden with these men tonight, or more likely he riled them up to do his dirty work. The man's no good, rotten to the core, but then again, ain't no coward either. What I'm tryin' to say, and failing to, is that he is slippery like a snake. There ain't no figurin' out a man like Hanley.'

'These raids always have this many riders? This was a small battle.'

'Nah, this was the worse one yet. Iffen you hadn't pulled that crazy stunt of yours we'd all be dead, lying here next to these men on the ground.'

'I just reacted to the situation,' Chisenhall said. 'I wasn't even thinking about what I did.'

'Maybe that is the case, but it was damn heroic, nonetheless. Crazy, maybe even foolish, but heroic,' Jack Allison replied. 'You seem to know how to handle those guns.'

'I was taught by my father, who learned in the war,' Chisenhall explained.

'I was in the war myself, but didn't see much if any action fortunately. The worst I've seen is holding this ranch against these night riders. And that has been just recently.'

When they had surveyed all the dead masked raiders, they discovered the faces of several men they recognized, but none they really knew well.

'That shows me that he has to go outside of this area to get men to do this type of work,' Allison said. 'Men around here don't want to do things like this.'

'Yet they still do nothing to stop him, either,' Chisenhall noted. 'Except for you and your men. You all should work together and join with the rest of the area to run Hanley out, get a good lawman to maintain peace in the area.'

'The men around these parts are mere farmers and ranchers, not gun hands.'

'So am I, and so are you,' Chisenhall reminded the man.

'Yeah, but you are different. I wouldn't guess you to be a farmer to look at you,' Allison remarked.

'You didn't seem like a mere farmer either, when the bullets began flying. Everyone in this town and area has something worth fightin' for. Once Hanley gets rollin' he'll buy out every one of you, and have all the power in these parts. Then he'll be even more dangerous.'

'Well, that may be. . . .'

'No wells, ifs, ands or buts, Allison. A man like Rake Hanley can always hire bad men to do his dirty work.' Chisenhall waved his rifle at the dead sprawled out on the ground. 'Men like these are plentiful out here in the west. Most of 'em have fled the east, running from crimes, and most are veterans of the war, prone to killin', accustomed to it even.

'There are good men out here too, don't get me wrong. Men like you, these men you got helpin' you. But they're not born killers. But you got to put an end to Hanley's raids, Allison.'

'I know, I know.'

'You can't expect them to stop by hidin' out here. Only going to get worse, now that you stood up against him. Hell, it may already be too late. Things may be out of control.'

'I can't just let him take my spread. I've put too much into working this land, just to give it up.'

'No one is sayin' to turn tail and leave what is rightfully yours. I'm sayin' do something about it. Try something else.'

Allison lifted the shotgun. 'This is the only thing I know to do. Like I said, there ain't no law around here. It's all we can do. The law doesn't care about me, these fellas, or Mesilla.'

'That's what I'm sayin'. You care. The other farmers care – because as soon as Hanley either runs you off or kills you, he'll move on to the next man, the next spread, and so on.

Band together as you did today and push back against Hanley.'

Jack Allison thought for a moment. 'You sound more reasonable than a man with vengeance on his mind. I thought you only cared about getting your pound of flesh from Hanley.'

'Well, I aim to do that, but I hate to see others suffer too. It just ain't right.'

'I admire that. You have been up front with me since I met you.'

'I just don't like to see good, hard-working men like yourself get railroaded by a man like Rake Hanley, it just ain't right. I want to do something to stop him.'

Allison smiled. 'Well, you most certainly stopped a few of his men tonight.'

'I reckon we stopped a few of them, but they'll be back with greater numbers, for sure. We got to stop them at the root. Bound to lose more men in the process, but at least it will be worth it. We need to get organized. If we can band together, we have a chance.'

'I'll talk to the men, try to convince them.'

'Let me drive the point home, Allison. You got Annie May to worry about. She's still young. They wounded her this time, but the next time they may kill her. What do you think would have happened to her tonight if Hanley's men had defeated you all?'

Allison's face darkened.

'I hate to imagine what they would have done,' Chisenhall added.

'I know you're right. Some of these boys came here from farms and ranches to help me take care of mine. But their places will be next, for sure.'

'Now you sound like you understand.'

'But some of these boys came against their wills. Their families didn't want them involved. They said it was my problem, and to stay out of it. Slate, over there, his family, they wanted him to stay the hell away from all of this. I don't blame them. Guess they were right after all. He's dead now. I have to tell them that. I wouldn't be surprised if they blamed me . . . I do.'

'No time for blame right now, other than for Hanley. This is his doing. You can console Slate's family later. You're got to work together, all of you, before it's too late.'

'First thing tomorrow, I'll talk to them,' Allison said. 'After I talk to the families of those who were killed tonight. Yeah, first thing right after that.'

Hanley's night riders were a ragged group now, shot up and much disheartened. They rode against the night, fast as hell at first, dreading that the devil with the blasting six-guns might be on their rear. They rode down pine-needled trails and across thin, winding creeks, on out to the old Wallace place, now the headquarters of Rake Hanley.

By the time they reached the farm, they were exhausted. They rode up to the house and dismounted, shed back their hoods and stepped up on the long, round porch.

Before they could say a word or enter, the door flew open and a large man edged in lantern light looked out at them. He was hatless, wore a night shirt stuffed in Confederate uniform pants, minus the stripe – which had faded away. The man had an extremely scarred face, and in his hand he held a revolver.

'You fellas sure got that done pretty quick.'

The man who seemed to be the leader of the riders spoke: 'Didn't go as planned. Got shot up.'

The big man looked out over the group of the once masked night riders.

'Lost some boys, did ya?'

'We did . . . several in fact.'

'Come on, Hanley, let us in. We're in bad shape.'

Rake Hanley turned his back on the men and went inside the cabin, the one he had seized from the Wallaces when they had opportunely decided to move. He went over to the rock fireplace and rested on the mantel. He put the revolver on it, just below where a sheathed sabre lay stretched across the mantel.

'All right, Bish,' Hanley said to the man who had addressed him before. 'Give it to me. What happened? It doesn't look good.'

'Well, we got two or three of them, Mr Hanley. The moon made it too light out for a decent shootin',' Bish Craig responded.

'I don't pay you for excuses, Bish. Go on and explain.'

'We did like you wanted. We tried to shoot the Allison place up, had those farmers on the run . . . we did . . . at least for a short time.' Bish paused.

'But what?' Hanley urged.

'They were fairly well organized, Mr Hanley, better than we expected.' The man called Bish Craig looked around at the other riders who were huddled near shoulder to shoulder, none of them making eye contact with Hanley.

'Out with it, you're holding out on me, Bish.'

'It appears Allison and those farmers hired themselves a professional gun hand,' Bish finally stated.

'A professional gun hand?'

'Yessir, that's right. A crazy man that can shoot like a marksman. He came chargin' out from behind that barricade of theirs riding a horse, guns blazin'. Took down some of our best men, right quick too.'

Hanley grinned an acerbic sort of sullen grin. 'Are you tellin' me that one man – professional gun hand or not – ran off you and twenty other men?'

'Weren't twenty at that time, some had fallen before that. So, it was less.' Bish Craig knew his answer did not help matters.

'Don't give me that lousy excuse. Is that what you want to stick with, really?'

'You didn't see him; he was like a man possessed. He rode and shot like no man I've ever seen before, Mr Hanley.'

'He was the devil hisself,' another of the men added.

'Shut up the lot of you!' Hanley barked furiously. 'You mean to tell me that one man ran all of you off with your tails tucked between your legs? What am I paying you all for? Why do I put my neck on the line robbing and stealing just to waste that money on men like you all? I need better men than you all, that much is certain now. Over twenty paid men were stopped by one man!'

'Wasn't exactly like that, Mr Hanley,' Bish began.

'Then how exactly was it, Bish? You all had more men, and more guns. So tell me why I shouldn't view you and these men as cowards?'

Bish Craig's look went taciturn. 'You should have been there with us then, Mr Hanley. Then maybe you could have taken care of this man yourself. You talk as big as you stand, Hanley.'

Hanley's hand flashed. He raised the pistol off the mantel swiftly, like a striking snake.

Bish went for his gun through the slit in his robe. He was too late.

The sound of Hanley's revolver was like the roar of a bear in that small room. The shot carried Bish back into the other men, his own gun firing off into the plank floorboards, throwing up dust and splinters.

Bish was caught by a few of the other men and carefully lowered to the floor.

'Pay attention,' Hanley announced, still holding the smoking revolver in his hand, 'we are going to reach an agreement right now. I'm the boss. I pay you, and it is more than any of you has made in the past year riding drag behind some herd or plowing fields.' He was snarling now through his yellowed, rotten teeth. 'If any of you here don't want to work for me, do the things I ask, you can leave now, no hard feelings, or you can take a slug just like Bish here.'

There was shocked silence in the room.

'Well, we have an agreement?' Hanley asked.

Not one of the men responded, but they all nodded.

'That's good,' Hanley said, 'because I would hate to have to waste more bullets on you.'

And with that he turned and spat on the body of Bish Craig.

CHAPTER 15

STRENGTHENING AND BUILDING

As the sun rose early and bright, a wagon carrying the bodies of the dead protectors and driven by Jack Allison himself, a shotgun rider alongside him, set out to return the bodies to their families. Allison left Chisenhall in charge, and gave precise orders for everyone to mind what he might ask them to do.

Chisenhall was a might awkward with this turn of events. He didn't set much store on being anyone's boss or leader, nor did he really like having a superior himself – which was why he ran his own farm. But as he was the one who had talked Allison into trying to build a council of the local men, and since Jack had combined that with the unpleasant undertaking of returning to their homes the bodies of those who had died protecting his spread, Chisenhall accepted it – reluctantly, but he accepted it nonetheless.

The first order he gave was to send a group of men, who were well armed, down to the nearby creek for stones and components for the fence and barricade. He wanted to strengthen the barricade, and also to increase its height, especially around the house, and build up a good fortification for the barn.

He also brought in the bulk of the farmstock and placed it within the limits of the wall. This included pigs, horses, a mule, two cows and a handful of chickens. Pens and coops had to be built, and this took a substantial amount of time – but at this season of the year, time was abundant. The crops, a few turnips and greens, took care of themselves, and were not so great a money maker anyway – who didn't have turnips? So there was no real time wasted, he reckoned.

The men stayed constantly on the alert for a surprise attack, but the work gave them something to keep their minds occupied, and their hands busy, too. Chisenhall knew this would help keep them from thinking about their fallen defenders and deciding to run off. He didn't really blame them if they had wanted to. As Jack Allison had said, they didn't have the revenge thing that he and Chisenhall had. But on another hand, as Chisenhall had explained to Allison last night, it was something that would eventually affect them all.

At about noon the men stopped their work when they heard a most welcome sound – the clanking of the dinner bell.

Chisenhall put down the large rock he had been carrying to the fence and pulled on his shirt. He went on up to the house to wash his face and hands.

A few of the men who had already eaten took their turns on guard duty while the others prepared to satisfy their hunger. Chisenhall waved at them as he passed their station atop the barn.

The men had made him something of a hero after the raid, and in a way that worried him deeply. He seemed to be tying strings to himself, and in order to do what he intended to do, he needed to be free of restraints. He felt as if his feet were entangled in underbrush. One commitment after another.

He had planned to come to Mesilla to kill Rake Hanley, to act out his revenge in cold blood and a hail of bullets, and here he was lugging rocks and sticks and waving at men under his command. It was a long way from the blind, emotionless killing in a Mesita del Gato brothel. He felt as if some of his emotions were coming back to life, still mostly buried deep inside him to near complete nothingness – but there was something stirring there again. Something that caused him significant pain.

Last night he had had a man, then another, and another. Men whose names he did not know and may never know. Men who threatened his life and the lives of the other men who garrisoned Jack Allison's ranch. And though he had thought little about it at the time as he killed one after another, firing into them and dropping them from their horses, this morning, when they had buried them on the upper slope of the spread, he had felt hurt for what he had done the night before. It was not regret, but hurting for having to take the lives of those men.

He steeled his thoughts back to that morning that four men came riding up to the grave he'd been digging for his wife, and then cast his mind on Hanley's sabre piercing the body of his boy clean through his chest and out his back.

Chisenhall clenched his teeth and strode quickly toward the house. After washing up at the bowl and stand outside, drying on the towel provided, he went into the long room that served as the dining area. The table was twelve feet long and heaped with food. The men were gathered about it, and surprising to him, Annie May was present too. She was seated, her wooden crutch propped on the back of her chair. The only empty chair happened to be the one next to her.

He could not help but enjoy that fact just a little. Chisenhall took the seat next to Annie May, and she smiled slightly to him. He smiled back. His smiles were becoming frequent again.

'I want to say thank you to you once more,' Annie May said.

He waved off her comments. 'I did nothing but happened upon you.'

'It was a good thing that you did,' she replied. 'Pa told me all about what you did before he left this morning.'

'I'm starving, can we just say our blessings and get to eatin'?' said a younger man, whose name Chisenhall had learned was Carter Banton.

'As I was the man who cooked this meal, I say dig in,' said another, heavier man whose name Chisenhall had yet to learn.

Annie May led the blessings and then they all got to eating, and it was most welcome and delicious. In between bites he found himself stealing glances at Annie May.

After the meal, the men, except for those already on guard duty, took an afternoon rest. Chisenhall, with Annie May leaning and hopping on her crutch, half using him for support, and wholly enjoying his arm around her waist, took to walking about the barricade.

'Should you be up and walking on that leg?' he asked her.

'I was taught not to favor an injury, or it could stove up on you,' she replied. 'At least that is what my pa says.'

'You do everything your pa says?'

She stopped and gave him a sharp look. 'Just about. Why? He's a good man.'

'I have no doubt about that,' he answered. 'Meant no offense, miss.'

They stopped at the far end of the barricade, and Annie May leaned her back against the wall and blew out her breath.

'It will take a bit to get used to using this crutch,' she noted.

'Well, hopefully you won't have to use it that much longer. I imagine you'll be sore for some time, but from how the wound looked the doc did a nice job in patching you up.'

At that revelation Annie May's face reddened.

'You saw me? You were there the whole time?'

He nodded.

'I kind of remember seeing your face, but honestly don't remember too much about that night. I was in and out a lot of the time,' she admitted.

'I was there, Doc needed help in treating you.'

'And you saw Doc Griffith cauterize the wound? And me?'

'Um . . . well . . .' Chisenhall felt his face getting warm. 'I did. As I said . . . Doc needed the help.'

Her cheeks were blushing red now.

'I hope I didn't embarrass you, miss. I mean . . .'

'Don't be silly. If the doc needed help and you were there, I wouldn't be here now. Thank you for helping to save me.'

'You're welcome.'

'What has you in this area, Mr Hall?' Annie May asked, changing the subject.

'Just passin' through, I guess. I'm a drifter . . . now helping out your pa. . . .'

She wasn't buying it. 'Uh huh. Pa says you are a good man. He's good at reading people, always has been.'

'That is mighty kind of him to say so.'

'He says that if it were not for you last night, those masked riders might've overrun us all. Said that you pretty much single handedly ran them off,' she said.

'He's makin' much more of what I did than what actually happened,' Chisenhall replied.

'Pa wasn't the only one saying that about you, either,' she noted. 'Many of the men say they owe their lives to you.'

'I hope they don't really think that. I don't want that responsibility. I was just trying to survive last night, same as the rest of the men. There's nothing special about me,' he responded.

'I doubt that, John Hall.'

Annie May calling him by his alias bothered Ross Chisenhall. He had not yet become accustomed to the new name, and somehow it seemed she should call him Chisenhall, or even Ross – that somehow that would put them on closer, more familiar terms. And at that moment, looking into her eyes, he wasn't certain that he wanted to get close to anyone, but if he did . . . it would definitely be Annie May Allison.

He realized he had been standing there looking awkwardly

at her for a few minutes now, and that neither of them had spoken.

'Let's walk some,' she finally said.

Chisenhall helped her away from the wall, and as he did, her crutch slipped and she fell forward into his arms, and her eyes – those deep blue eyes – were staring into his own. Her mouth parted, and his lips went to hers as if pushed from behind. The two kissed long and gently.

When he quickly drew back from her, his arms still around her, he looked panicked. 'I am so sorry, Miss Allison! I shouldn't have done that.'

'No . . . it's . . . all right,' she stammered.

He tried to smile, but cursed himself inwardly at allowing him to get this close. Had he betrayed his wife?

He had one of the other men repair her crutch as he helped her the rest of the way back to the house, where he left her to finish strengthening the barricade.

CHAPTER 16

A DARKNESS INSIDE

By the end of the day Jack Allison returned looking bone weary and beaten down.

The barricade had been completed and the men were about to eat dinner, a simple meal of cornbread and beans. Chisenhall gave them approval to break for supper, and as they all made their way to the house, he went over to Allison, who was very slowly climbing down from the wagon. One of the guards swung up into the wagon's seat and drove it on to the barn to unharness, feed and water the horses.

'You look to have had one long day,' Chisenhall noted.

'It's extremely difficult to look the families of those men in the eyes and explain to them they will never see them again,' Allison said, frowning.

Chisenhall nodded his agreement, then added, 'I reckon that is about one of the hardest things to do, no doubt.'

'Just the blank stares they returned to me . . .'

'Reckon they won't have trouble looking at you when Hanley's raiders turn their guns on their ranches.'

'I reckon not.'

'Did you bring up creating a council or joining together?'

'Not one of the families of those dead men wanted anything

to do with me, nor did they speak to me. And I can't say as I blame them at all.'

'I reckon they'll have to move on soon enough, whether they want to or not.' As he said those words he thought: But I didn't . . . But that's different. Completely different.

'Some of the others showed a little interest in the notion. I talked to many folks today, John, and didn't come near covering all the farms – only those I could get to today. Some of them are going to speak to the others, see what they can get going.'

'How long will that take?' Chisenhall asked.

'Maybe know something tomorrow night. Told 'em to come here, as it would be safer. Hopefully we can all come to some kind of understanding.'

'Worth a try, I reckon. They have to see the sense in doing so. You'd all be stronger as a combined group.'

Allison sighed. 'The folks around here are different, I suppose, John. They just want to be left alone to tend to their farms, and ranch the way they want to. They don't much like being told what to do.'

'Most people don't. And what they want, is that all you want?'

'Yeah, it is. But right now, the sights of Hanley's guns are aimed at me and my property – and that doesn't sit well with me,' Allison explained.

'Those sights will be aimed at each one of them soon enough.'

'But unfortunately it may take that for some around here to see for themselves what's truly going on.'

'It may be too late for them then. Hanley will have taken their farms from each one of them by that time.'

'I believe that. And I know what you say is the truth. Let's hope we can get them to agree with us that we need to band together to become strong enough to oppose Hanley.'

'All you can do is try,' Chisenhall said.

'That we can. I tell you what, John, I was at the end of my rope today . . . about to throw in the towel and take Annie May far away from this area – and then I spoke to you. Thanks.'

Chisenhall wasn't sure if that was a compliment or not. 'Maybe you should take her and get back on that wagon and skedaddle. Who knows for sure?'

'I understand.'

The two men stood in silence for a moment, then finally Jack Allison said: 'C'mon, let's go on up and get some dinner before the others eat it all.'

A few hours after supper, Annie May walked with Chisenhall – using a makeshift cane now instead of the crutch – out to hay down the horses. Most of the men had gone to sleep, though of course there were guards posted to cover all angles.

The two talked as Chisenhall finished his chore, and then they went outside in the light of the stars and the moon, and leaned against the wall barricade, which was just about six feet in height now. Without speaking, the two made their way to a darkened corner near the barricade.

'Not sure if this will be enough,' he said as he placed his hand on the fortification.

'John . . . we need to . . . uh . . . talk.'

'Thought that's what we've been doing,' he said, trying to be funny.

She smiled politely. 'You know what I mean.'

'Look, I haven't gotten over the death of my family . . . my wife . . . this happened all of a sudden . . . I didn't mean. . . .'

'Real sudden, for sure,' she agreed.

'I don't want to lead you on. . . .'

'You haven't . . . John . . . it's OK . . . I don't want to place any pressure on you.'

'I appreciate that.'

'I can see that you have things that you have to do. Things that have your attention more than I do right now.'

He grunted. She had no idea.

'I'm not a foolish little girl, John.'

'Annie May. . . .'

'Annie, please, my pa is the only one that calls me Annie May . . . at least I think he's the only one,' she said.

'Annie . . . like I said . . .'

'It's fine, you do what you have to, I will be here. I don't want you to rush into this, not with you still reeling from your wife's death and all.'

Pause. 'You know I do like you, Annie M . . . um . . . Annie. But I do have . . . um . . . things – as you put it – that I need to do.'

'And I won't stop you.'

'You may if you only knew,' he muttered. He wasn't sure if she had heard him or not.

'So tell me. . . .' She had heard.

He vigorously shook his head.

'Does it have to do with your family? Your wife?'

'Yes, as a matter of fact, it does. But it's not a story that I wish to relive. . . .'

She moved to him and slipped her arm around his waist, and he responded, but removing the arm and stepping away. It wasn't that he didn't like it, the problem was he liked it too much.

'It happened not all that long ago. . . .' He began without looking at her. '. . . There was this farmer. He was married with two children – a girl and a boy. He was happy, and loved his family a great deal. His wife was a wonderful woman. She stuck by him through the harsh winters and blistering summers, money or no money, and always seemed happy. She gave him two wonderful children. Then without warning, sickness took the girl, the oldest child. Not long after that the same sickness came for her – his wife.

'As he and his boy were digging her grave, four riders rode up to them on his farm. They killed the little boy, and they buried the man alive – but he lived, and he got out of that grave and he went after those men.

'He went sort of mad, caught up with one of them, killed him in cold blood. The man is most likely wanted by the law for doing so. Before he killed that first man, though, he forced him to tell him where to find the other three. Some of that vengeful lust is gone, but the hate and the pain still linger. The only thing that will dull the pain is killing those men. No matter how long it takes him, he will find those other men, and one by one. . . .'

'I'm so sorry that happened to you, John,' Annie May said.

He did not respond. She moved a step away from him. 'I can hear that you still love her . . . your wife, I mean.'

'I do.'

'Does that mean you cannot love me?'

'I don't know. I do still love her. . . .'

'What was her name?'

'Caroline. I said I loved her still, but maybe it's her memory that I still love.'

'A memory? Will a memory comfort you at night? Does that mean . . . ?'

'I don't know, Annie . . .' He was hurting now. The memories of Caroline, Katy and Johnny flooding his mind. 'A memory can't comfort me, least not the ones of them. But they do haunt me.'

'For how long will they?'

'Until my vengeance is fulfilled, I reckon.'

Annie May wrapped her arms around herself. She paused, then she spoke. 'Your children? What were their names?'

'Katy and Johnny. . . .' Tears rolled down his cheeks.

'How long ago did this happen, John?'

'Not even two weeks ago.'

'Oh, dear Lord, you poor man. Your wife's dead less than two weeks and I'm out here in the moonlight pouring my desires on you. I'm so sorry, John.'

'You didn't know. And frankly, Annie . . . you have helped. I can't live forever with the pain of those events, with their deaths much longer. But I can't seem to move past that pain and my anger toward those men, either. Do you understand?'

'I think I do. I was mad when my mother died. Mad at my dad, mad at the whole world. She was taken by a sickness too, John.'

'Please, stop calling me John. I can't pretend that is my name any more. I'm sorry. It isn't my true name. I lied, as I wasn't sure if I was a wanted man or not. . . .'

She stopped, turned slightly to look him in the face. 'What is your name?'

'Ross. Ross Chisenhall.'

'Ross – I like it. I didn't think you looked like a John.'

'Reckon I best inform your pa that I lied to him . . . unless . . . you think I ought not to?'

'You afraid the law is after you still?'

'The law, bounty hunters, the man's brothers, you name it.'

'How long can you keep running from them?'

'I don't know.'

'What if you never go back?'

'I would be dogged to the ends of the earth, I reckon. Someone is bound to catch up to me sooner or later. I couldn't ask you or anyone to live with that sort of pressure.'

'Ross, for you, I would. . . .'

'Please don't finish that sentence. You don't know me well enough . . .' he paused. 'Not yet.'

'Does that mean you love me?'

He did not say anything, but she saw it in his eyes. She flashed a quick smile. His look then changed to one that she thought was anger.

'Are you mad?'

He nodded. 'But not at you.'

'Why?'

'This . . . complicates things.'

'How so?'

'I can't stay here, Annie. I'm pushing my luck as it is. I'm putting you in even more danger.'

'You've changed your name,' she started. 'Doesn't that mean you can stay and be that new man? Forget the past?'

'Maybe. But I've got to go back. I made a promise to my wife and my children. I made it at their graves. I promised to Johnny that the man who put him in a grave would pay for that.'

Annie May reached out and touched Chisenhall's face, tracing her fingers along the crescent-shaped scar.

'The same man gave you this?'

'Yes. And I'm glad. It serves as a reminder.' His tone was cold again.

She followed the scar from the bottom to the top. It was more a laceration of the soul than one of the flesh. She knew that now, and appreciated the darkness it had released. The same darkness that would take him away from her.

'It would not be right for me to ask you to go back on your promises, or to forget,' she said softly. 'I can ask that you come back after you have gotten your vengeance. Please, don't forget me.'

He was hurt by that, but only somewhat. 'I could never forget you, Annie.'

She hugged him and the two said nothing as the embrace lasted a few minutes.

He took her in his arms, held her tight, and placed his lips on hers for a short-lived beautiful moment – and then her voice whispered in his ear: 'Love me, Ross. Love me now.'

'Here?' He was shocked.

'Yes, here and now.'

'Annie . . . I can't make any promises to you now. Not even that I can come back alive.'

'That is why I want you to love me now, Ross.' She went in for another kiss, he turned away. His gaze turned into the wall and then to the ground, into the shadows, and it was like looking inside himself.

They were there in the melodious darkness for a brief time, a darkness that Chisenhall hoped did not take Annie May, but knew it most likely would consume him.

Later that night, snug in his bedding, Chisenhall thought of Annie May's warm, sweet embrace, and of how it had killed the winter chill in the air and burned away at the coldness of his heart.

There were still things he had to do. Things that if left undone would haunt him for the rest of his life and rattle in his head like chains.

But maybe, just maybe he could come back to Annie and live like a man on the run, and her live like a fugitive's wife.

That was stupid. No. It was best he rode out of her life after he had evened the score with Rake Hanley. Just rode on, far away. No word. No goodbye. Nothing of the sorts. Nothing that might give her a glimmer of hope to hang on to. Just up and disappear. That was the answer. That was the way to handle this. Let her not cling to false hopes and dreams. The memory of him would fade away in time. She was young enough that she would recover.

But would he?

That night Chisenhall slept and dreamed again, but this time the dreams were of Annie May and her loving embrace, and there was no horror in the dreams. The dreams brought some comfort to him.

And for the first time in over a week, he awoke after a good night's rest, fully refreshed.

BOOK FOUR

THE RECKONING

CHAPTER 17

DAMN GOOD AT KILLING

They met in Allison's barn that next night, nearly twenty ranchers and farmers from places from around the area. Not a one seemed very happy about being there at that moment. They sat on hay bales and machinery with wariness and fear in their eyes.

'You know why I have called you all here tonight,' Jack Allison started. 'And by the way, where is Old Luke? He promised he would be here.'

'Lots of people aren't here, Jack,' a gangling rancher named Nat Martin said. 'I sorta wish I hadn't come, either.'

'Well,' Allison said, glowering, 'Luke wanted to be here. He's sixty years old and he's more a man than the lot of you, that's no lie.'

'Now wait a cotton-pickin' minute. . . .' Martin began.

'No. You wait a cotton-pickin' minute.' The man who had spoken was tall and dark with a long, silver scar on his cheek. He sported a revolver on each hip and two crossed in his waistband. There was something vicious about the look in his eyes, like a caged or trapped animal, ready to burst in a fury of rage.

106

'Just who the hell are you?' Martin asked, but his heart wasn't behind the words, and his tone went weak. He took a seat quickly and hoped no one had heard.

They all had.

'My name is John Hall. Friend of Mr Allison's. I work for him. I got me a personal stake in this situation. I am no admirer of Rake Hanley, you can be damned sure of that.'

'I don't know any of us here that are,' a man yelled from the back.

'Then I suggest we listen then, instead of talking,' Annie May called out. She had slipped in unnoticed by the men. 'Hear what my father and – and John have to say to you all.'

'You've all come all the way out here to Mr Allison's place,' Chisenhall said. 'You did that much, least you could do to make it worth your while is to listen.'

'Agreed,' another farmer shouted. 'Ain't gonna hurt us any to listen.'

Voices muttered in agreement.

Allison said, 'Good – now listen up, men. This is my place and it's in Hanley's sights right now. But once he's done with me, who's next?'

'Maybe he'll stop with your place,' Martin said.

'Could be,' Allison replied. 'But I can't see that he'd be satisfied with just my place. Can't understand you being OK with it if he was.'

Nat Martin stood up. 'Allison, you're a good man. I know you need our help. You've done a lot for me in the past, I can't speak for anyone else – for all of us, for that matter, from what I've heard. But I just have a tiny place, hardly enough to eat off. My wife is ill. You know how sickly Betty is, and she's expectin' a baby soon. Nothing Hanley could want or do with that tiny old place of ours. It ain't even got good soil. It might be a tad selfish, but it's my place and my family I'm thinking of.'

'Now wait a minute,' Annie May said. 'Listen to yourself, Nat Martin. Listen real good to what you just said.'

'I ain't got to listen to some woman,' snapped Martin.

'She's got as much a right to speak as any of you,' Chisenhall said. 'Now shut up for a moment, Martin, you've said your piece.'

Martin moistened his lips with a quick swipe of his tongue across them and was silent.

'You're letting Hanley cut off the head of your group,' Annie May went on. 'It's no secret that my pa has the biggest spread in these parts. The other good farms and ranches have already been taken by Hanley. You small farmers and ranchers are just next in line for the chopping block. When they cut off the head, the rest of the body dies quickly. But my pa's got plenty of bite left in him.'

'You sayin' we're yellow, missy?' Martin asked.

'If you don't fight back against Hanley, then yes, that's exactly what I'm sayin'.'

'I just explained that I have a sick wife who's expectin' a baby at home. . . .'

'Excuses. You know, Hanley won't stop with taking my pa's place – yours and the others are next. That is what Hanley will do, there's no denying it. He wants all of Mesilla, and will take it one way or another from each of you, sick and pregnant wives or not,' Annie May went on.

'We could just pack up and go,' Martin said.

'You can,' Allison responded. 'You can run. Each and every one of you can run. But that won't save your places. Then you go somewhere else and start over. Maybe things will be better there, maybe not. Maybe there are other Hanleys. And if there aren't, how can you call yourselves men if you run?'

'It sounds to me,' said one of the men who had spoken up before, 'it's you that's in trouble here, and you need our help.'

A mumble of agreement followed the man's words.

'All right, all right,' Allison said loudly. 'I've never said anything different. Yes, I need your help right now. Without it I haven't a chance against Hanley and his masked riders. I may be able to hold them off for a little bit, but they'll just keep coming and eventually overrun me. I have men on the lookout right now, expecting another raid any time. That isn't a way to live. I shouldn't have to worry about raids at all hours of the day and night. I'm a farmer, just like most of you. But once they do overtake me and my place, they'll just move on to the next and the next.'

'We ought to be able to depend on our friends, and they ought to be able to depend on us for the same,' Annie May added.

'How do we know you'll be there if the situation was reversed?' asked Martin.

'Have I ever let any one of you men down when you needed my help?'

No one said anything in response.

'Here is the simple truth,' Chisenhall said. 'If you all band together, you can run Hanley and his thugs out of town. No more raids from his masked riders, and no more sleepless nights wondering if they're goin' to ride down on you and your families. Oh, you may not be wondering that right now, as all sights seem to be on Mr Allison's place at the moment, but you will soon. As one place falls, the next is already being targeted. And Jack can't hold the raiders off much longer. Barricade, guards or none at all. Hanley will simply keep bringing in gun hands to replenish those he loses until he has all of your ranches and farms.'

Allison spoke now. 'All I am askin' of you men is to consider what has been said here today and. . . .'

Suddenly he was interrupted by a man running into the barn. It was Rory Cabot, one of his ranch hands. 'Mr Allison, come quick, it's Old Luke. You best hurry. He's hurt real bad.'

At a run the men were out of the barn, Jack Allison leading them.

A wagon was pulled up in front of the main house, and slumped in its seat, barely hanging on, was Luke Cochran.

Allison rushed to the old man and put a hand on his arm.

'Don't pull my arm away,' Luke Cochran advised. 'It's all that's holding in my innards.'

Allison felt something warm and wet on his hand. It was blood.

'Good Lord, Luke, what happened?' Allison asked.

'Those damn masked fools. One of my hands. That boy I hired on to help me fix the barn the other day . . . you know the boy. . . .'

'Save your strength, Luke,' Allison said. 'John, let's bed him down in the back of the wagon and take him in to Doc Griffith.'

Chisenhall swung up on the wagon beside Cochran. 'We'll take it slow and easy, OK? We're goin' move you to the back of the wagon,' he said. 'Think you can do that?'

'I'm not sure, mister, I'm cut pretty deep. It's real bad, son. Got my innards in my hand, just my shirt and my hand holding them in,' the old man said, his face pale from the loss of blood.

'We're gonna try to get you on your back, Luke,' Allison said sliding up on the other side of the old man.

Chisenhall took one shoulder beneath his arm, scooped up Old Luke's legs with the other as Allison took the opposite side. Fortunately for them Cochran was small and not a heavy man, and easily lifted into the back of the wagon.

'I'll get some bedding,' Annie May said, and ran for the house.

'Christ almighty!' Luke Cochran cried out. 'They done killed me.'

'You'll be all right, Luke,' Allison said unconvincingly. 'Hang in there, old man.'

'I'm not sure that I can, Jack,' Cochran replied.

A few minutes later, Annie May returned with a thick blanket and a pillow. Allison put the pillow under Cochran's head and covered him with the blanket.

'Sorry that we can't make you a more comfortable ride,

Luke,' Allison apologized.

Old Luke made a mewing sound in his throat.

'Get goin',' Allison said to Chisenhall.

'This is what happens when we go stickin' our noses in other people's businesses,' Nat Martin said. 'They get cut off.'

'You're a damn coward, Martin,' Chisenhall snapped. 'Now get the hell out of the way or I'll run you over with this team and wagon. Martin, give me a reason.'

'Good God, mister, Good God,' Martin said stepping back from the wagon.

'If anything,' Chisenhall said cracking the whip over the wagon's team, 'this should be the convincing you all need. This old man wasn't even on Allison's place. Think what could be goin' on at your places.'

'I'm comin' with you,' declared Annie May.

'Well jump up quickly,' Chisenhall said. 'I'd much rather have you with your pa and me than leave you here with these cowards.'

Annie May jumped up as the wagon was moving, took a rifle that was there from its boot, and put it across her lap.

'Rory,' Allison snapped. 'Open up the gate. And take charge. The rest of you yellow-bellied cowards can get off my land!'

'Get the hell out of the way or I will run you down, I swear to heaven,' Chisenhall added to the gathering throng of ranchers.

They split, creating a path, the gate opened, and Chisenhall drove out of the barricade deliberate and calm, trying to make a comfortable ride for the injured man, but also knowing he had to get him to the doctor quickly.

'Let me tell you what happened,' Old Luke said to Allison as they bounced along the road.

'Save your strength, Luke. You can tell me later. That cut is bad, you'll need your strength for the trip to Doc Griffith's,'

Allison replied.

'I'll be gone before we get to Doc Griffith's. You know it, and so do I. No sense in sayin' anything else, Jack. And you know I am right.'

'I don't know any such thing. So why are we wasting the time in driving you there, then?'

Old Luke tried to smile. 'OK, sure, Jack. Sure.'

'Now save that strength of yours,' Allison said.

'Listen to me, Jack. That boy I hired, Alan Brennan. He's one of Hanley's.'

'One of the masked riders?' Allison said shocked.

'That's it. Knew he was a drifter with a past that I cared not to know too much about, but I thought maybe he was goin' to be a fine hand. Guess since your spread borders mine, they thought they'd sneak a spy in on to my place. Probably wished that's how they handled yours in the first place. Maybe they have for all we know,' Luke said.

'All my help are local fellas, Luke. I'm safe there, I swear it,' Allison assured the old man.

Old Luke licked his lips. 'Well, when you stopped by my place the other day, talked to me about the meeting, and all. I reckon this boy, Brennan, overheard our conversation, or just put the pieces together. Anyway, he went and told Hanley. I think he meant to set an example by me – Hanley, that is.

'I'd barely left my place when them masked fools came out of the path on both sides of me. About twelve, I reckon. Maybe more, who knows for sure. I tried to put up a fight, and I think I winged one of 'em, but they came up on my blind side and jumped me. Pulled me right off the wagon and tied me to one of the wheels. Can you believe that, I was tied to my own wagon wheel, Jack? Don't that beat all? They took turns punching and kicking me, like it was some sort of game to them.

'I recognized one of them by his boots. They was them fancy things that kid Brennan liked and wore, and I said to them "Brennan, that you?" – just like that, plain as I said it to you.

112

And he pulled back his hood, not worried about showing his face at that moment. Then one of the others pulled out a big knife and knelt before me and went to work on me.'

Allison looked down, tears in his eyes.

Old Luke continued. 'One of those boys, probably their leader, not Hanley, mind you, I could tell it wasn't his voice – told the fella with the big knife to cut me so I'd die slowly, didn't want me to die quickly. Said he wanted me to learn a lesson, Jack.'

'Oh Lord,' Annie May murmured.

'Only regret I have is that I didn't take one of them fools with me, Jack,' Old Luke said with a faint smile.

'This is my fault, Luke,' Allison said.

'Now don't go blamin' yourself, Jack. Now I'm gonna listen to you and shut my mouth, die in quiet peace,' Cochran spoke, his voice weakening with each word.

'Listen here, Luke, you ain't gonna die, but you can shut your mouth,' Allison said with a wink to the old man. 'I'm frankly tired of listening to you.'

They rode on awhile in complete silence, Chisenhall, Annie May and Allison on high alert.

Chisenhall felt bad for having allowing Annie May to come with them out here in the dark and open with masked riders looming in the night, for now he feared they were probably waiting for them. But Allison hadn't objected, and Chisenhall thought the same thing might have went through Jack's mind that had went through his. Those men back at his place were pretty rattled, maybe even Allison's hands were too, and if the masked riders should decide to attack, who's to stop them? And with Annie May there by herself – well, it could be his own past all over again. A loved one lost. Chisenhall hoped he was underestimating those ranchers and farmers, but fear had a way of making a man do stupid things. It wasn't that he thought the men were truly malicious. But if Hanley were to promise to leave their places alone for the Allison spread, they just might take him up on the offer, and. . . .

A gun shot that tore up the wood on the side of the wagon shook him out of his thoughts and brought his left hand with his revolver in it up and ready to fire swiftly.

'In the back,' Chisenhall ordered Annie May. 'And keep your head down. Give the rifle to your father.'

Allison took the rifle, dropped and bellied up to the side of the wagon, almost where the bullet had exploded through the wood and plowed across to the other side. The wagon offered about as much protection against bullets as a bush.

Another shot flashed and the sound of a gun barked at the same time. More wood flew, and this time it was right where Annie May had been sitting.

Chisenhall snapped off a few quick shots in the general direction of the shot, and slouching down, whipped the team up. He heard Cochran groan as the wagon rocked forward.

'Hang on, Luke,' Allison said.

'Just whip the hell out of those nags,' Old Luke responded.

And now the masked riders came out of their element, four of them. A select party that had been placed on the road to hit anyone coming from Jack Allison's spread by night.

Chisenhall abruptly pulled the horses to a stop and stood up in the wagon seat.

'What are you doin'?' Allison yelled. 'Are you insane?'

But a bullet ripped past his ear, and he bent down, bobbing up instantly to pump two shots toward the oncoming riders.

'More on this side, too,' Annie May shouted, and three more riders came up on her side. She got off a shot from her father's pistol, and luckily, she hit one of them and he toppled from the saddle. The others rode toward the wagon screaming from behind their masks like wild men.

Chisenhall's revolvers jumped in his hands a couple of times, for now he held one in each hand, and he dropped two of the riders.

Chisenhall next jumped down from the wagon and began to

run toward the remaining riders on his side, screaming louder than the riders bearing down on Annie May.

Annie May very coolly targeted one of the riders, and as wood splintering up into her face, she fired blindly.

The masked rider's horse went down. It had yanked its head up just as she fired and had taken the bullet through the brain. The masked rider rolled and got up in a swift move – but only for a moment, as Annie May's next shot – which was not fired blindly – knocked him down as her slug entered his right eye. He did not get up a second time.

Allison took careful aim and dropped one of the riders that the crazy man with the revolvers was running at, still screaming wildly at the top of his lungs. When it came to killing, this John Hall – as he knew him – didn't show much common sense against odds, but he was lucky, or just damn good, or both.

Chisenhall, with his left revolver, shot one of the horsemen in the chest, spun over with the right revolver and gave him another bullet for the hell of it.

The remaining masked rider set low on his horse and came straight for Chisenhall.

Chisenhall placed the right revolver in his holster, tossed his left to his right and took careful aim. When the horse's head tossed ever so slightly, Chisenhall shot it through the neck, and the slug went through the animal and into the stooping masked rider's jaw.

The horse went down skidding, throwing up hunks of turf with its knees. Blood foamed from its mouth and the hole in its neck.

Chisenhall hated to kill the horse, but it was a good shot nonetheless, or just a lucky shot as the rider passed, and Chisenhall didn't care either way.

The masked rider flew off the horse and hit the ground, tried to get up, and scraped along crablike. Blood dripped from beneath his hood, splashing on the ground.

Chisenhall took three brisk steps forward and shot the man

in the back of the head, without a second thought.

He then walked calmly back to the wagon. Jack Allison and Annie May were up on their knees, looking at him in shock.

'You don't care much for survivors, do you, John?' Allison questioned.

'When I start a job, I like to see it through to the end,' Chisenhall replied coolly.

'That is pretty clear, son,' Allison replied.

'What about the bodies?'

'What about them?' Chisenhall said. 'We got to get Luke to the doc, don't we? The hell with them fellas.'

CHAPTER 18

THERE IS ALWAYS HOPE

That night Annie May had seen the dark side, the side that lurked behind the eyes of the man she now knew to be Ross Chisenhall, alias John Hall. Not the Ross Chisenhall that night in the shadows of the wall, nor the Chisenhall that night of the rain, but the vengeful Chisenhall. The Chisenhall with the scar on his face and on his soul. The one who remembered clearly that day down by the graveside when four men had insulted the funeral of his wife and daughter, and killed his son and buried him alive.

She shivered just thinking about how he had stood up in the wagon, how he had jumped down and went to meet them. It did not occur to her, at least at the moment, that Chisenhall could have been killed. It was as if he were invincible. The very Angel of Death out to gather fallen souls.

It was a terrible side, but without it, they might not be here, might not be able to speculate.

No. Ross Chisenhall was a killer all right, no question about it, but not without cause. It was just that when he decided to do the job, he did it real efficient, especially for someone who only a few weeks earlier was not accustomed to such work. No riders to make their way back to Hanley and warn him that they were on their way to town. No one to tell Hanley to set up a big ambush with odds so great against them that even Chisenhall would fall before their lead amid smoke and thunder.

Ross Chisenhall was a man who had taken on a job and taken it to heart.

But there was more to him than that, and for a while she remembered those soft moments they had shared in the shadows of the wall.

Just before they got to Mesilla, Chisenhall looked back to those in the back of the wagon and said, 'I'm gonna try to pull in behind Doc Griffith's. Is there a way I can do that easily?'

'Yes, go straight on in like normal, but there's a small rut you can follow. That's how Doc takes his wagon out,' Jack Allison informed him.

'That's what I'll do.'

Chisenhall followed the trail until it turned to the main street, and then, when the lights of the saloon had come into focus, he came to the small rutted side trail – just two ruts in the road in actuality – and pulled up the wagon behind the doctor's place.

Annie May jumped out of the wagon and ran to knock on the sawbones' door. The cantankerous old doctor answered with his spectacles down on his nose and a book in his hands.

'Quick, it's Old Luke,' Annie May said. 'He's hurt pretty bad, Doc.'

Doc Griffith looked up to see Chisenhall and Allison unloading the injured man from the back of the wagon, carrying him up to the door.

'Make sure that door stays open, Annie May,' Doc Griffith said. 'You seem to have healed damn well and good.'

'Thanks to these two men,' she said.

'I reckon.'

'And you, of course, Doc,' she added.

118

'Thanks. Now get Luke in here pronto!'

Chisenhall and Allison carried Luke Cochran in through the doc's bedroom and into the front room where they put him on the wooden platform.

'He's hurt real bad, Doc,' Allison said. 'He's out cold now.'

'Shot?' the doc asked.

Chisenhall shook his head in response. 'They gutted him. He's been holding them in with his hand. This old fella is one tough son-of-a-gun.'

'I reckon he is,' Doc Griffith said. 'Light those lamps for me, and be damn quick about it, John.'

Chisenhall did as he was instructed, learning better and better the false name he had given himself, but liking it less and less also. He wanted to tell everyone who he really was, just as he had with Annie May. But it seemed hardly the right time to do that.

After lighting the lamps, Chisenhall went to the curtain and glanced out. A large number of horses were tied outside the saloon.

'Bet that's a group of Hanley's "friends",' Chisenhall noted.

Jack Allison came over to the window and looked out. 'Who else? No decent person can go in that saloon any more. Used to stop in for a drink myself now and then, but as I said, decent folk can't have a beer without rubbin' elbows with Hanley's ruffians.'

About that time a man came out of the saloon and stood on the porch. Before long, a saloon girl, pleasingly curvy and drunker than most cowboys after months on the trail, came out on the porch with him. They staggered and wobbled against each other, both using the other for some sort of support.

'Well, let it be known that Old Luke was right,' Allison said. 'That's the Brennan kid. The one Luke told me about. He worked for Old Luke. Was really one of Hanley's men all the time, I'll be damned!'

'Looks as if Hanley is branching out. It will be this whole

damn town and everything around it 'fore too long,'
Chisenhall remarked.

'Already is his town,' the doc said from the table where he
was cutting Cochran out of his shirt.

Chisenhall and Allison turned to see an ugly, jagged wound
in Cochran's belly, his guts sticking through it like a nest of
snakes.

'On my God!' Allison yelped.

Annie May, for all her toughness, stepped rapidly out back.
They could hear her getting sick.

Allison then said, 'I will make that Brennan kid pay for this.'
And he started for the door.

'Hold on there, Jack,' Chisenhall said. 'You'll have the
whole lot of Hanley's men to contend with.'

'Then I'll just have the whole goddamned lot to contend
with. I've just about had all that I can stand. No . . . I've had all
I can take.'

'Now hold on,' Doc Griffith said. 'It don't do you any good
to go out there and get yourself killed too. I've only got the one
table, Jack.'

'Those bastards are right there, drinkin' it up and laughin',
whorin', and not an hour or so ago a few of them tried to do
us in on the trail, and not long before that, Brennan told 'em
that Old Luke was coming out to my spread for a meetin' and
they jumped him, cut him open like a fish.'

Doc Griffith was about to work, but still he spoke evenly,
asked: 'What meeting?'

Allison explained swiftly, irascibly. In the midst of explain-
ing, Annie May returned. Chisenhall went over to her and put
his arms around her shoulders. 'I wouldn't look, if I were you.'

'Not to worry, I don't want to see that ever again. I won't
look. I asked to come with you all. I got no right to get sick at
a time like this,' she said.

'Nothing to be sorry for,' Doc Griffith said. 'Please put some
water on and tell your pa to shut his mouth and not to even

think about going over to the saloon.'

'Pa! You wouldn't think of doin' that, would you?' Annie May replied. 'Not by yourself?'

'If he decides to go over there,' Chisenhall said, 'he wouldn't be by himself.'

'You'll both be killed! It's suicide.' The girl's words hit home. She paused. 'At least go back to our place and get some men, if you have to go over. But not just the two of you.'

'So I'm forced to depend on other men now? This is my fight – and I guess John's here. We're the ones that got the highest stakes. Maybe we're the ones that ought to go up against Hanley and his men,' reasoned Allison.

'But it shouldn't be just the two of you,' Doc Griffith said calmly. 'Try that, and there won't be no one to look after Annie May here 'cept Hanley.'

Jack Allison's eyes widened. 'Now Doc, you've got no. . . .'

'The doc is correct,' Chisenhall said. 'Our best bet is to hope them farmers get some sense and band together.'

Allison let his breath out. 'Way they was talkin' and actin' tonight, I wouldn't count on them.'

'Give 'em a little more time, Jack,' Chisenhall replied. 'Then if they don't have the guts or mind to get on with it, you and I, and any other man you got that will stand with us, will come into town to see those boys over at the saloon.'

'And in the meantime, those masked riders will burn down your house, destroy your crops,' Doc Griffith said. 'Hanley has you in a tough spot, for sure, Jack.'

'I reckon that settles this then, don't it?'

'Jack,' Doc Griffith said, 'let me get Old Luke here patched up, and maybe the three of us can do something.'

'Three?' asked Allison. 'Doc, this ain't your fight.'

'I count four of us,' Annie May chimed in.

'Oh no you don't,' Doc Griffith said. 'I need you to stay and look after Luke.'

'Now just hold your horses – forgive me, Annie May,'

Chisenhall said.

'Don't give me that,' Annie May replied. 'Speak your mind.'

'Well, Doc, iffen you go and get yourself shot up, or worse, killed, who's the town supposed to depend on?'

'There won't be a town left not too long from now. Just will be Hanley and his masked riders,' the doctor offered.

'Still, who's gonna patch us up when we get shot up?'

The sawbones ignored that last question. 'We can just go down that street and go into that saloon and face down however many men Hanley has assembled over there and at least take a few of 'em with us. But when it's all over, we ain't gonna need any doctorin'. We may require an undertaker, that's for sure.'

'We may be able to take more of them than you think,' Allison said. 'Why, I've seen John here shoot the hell out of a bunch of those masked fools already. He's one helluva. . . .'

'I bet. He looks a tad crazy, if you ask me, just look at him. But you aren't going to go in no crowded saloon, surrounded by those ruffians, and come out of there alive. That won't solve anything. But if you insist on doing that foolish thing, I am going to be right there beside you boys. I can't let you go at it alone,' Doc Griffith said.

'Jack,' Chisenhall began, 'Doc has a point. I'll say this: we check out what those farmers and ranchers have decided, and then, no matter what, we either ride back here tomorrow night, or we go on out to where Hanley lives and hides himself away and we settle this once and for all.'

Jack Allison rubbed his chin. 'I don't like that Brennan kid walkin' around like nothin' happened.' He went over to the window and pulled the curtain back. Brennan and the girl were no longer in sight. That made the decision a tad easier to swallow. 'But I reckon what you say makes sense. Let's just hope those other boys decide in our favor.'

'There is always hope,' Doc Griffith added.

CHAPTER 19

DECISIONS AND CHOICES

They decided against returning by nightfall for fear of encountering more masked riders on the trail. They had been lucky earlier, but luck might not be on their side again.

Their decision was to wait until daybreak, and then light out, as they figured the Hanley riders would have cashed in their chips by that time after a night of gambling, boozing and such. As for those on the trail, well, it didn't appear that they were so well organized as to hit both night and day. Up until now they had hidden their faces and restricted themselves to the night.

Of course, they could be wrong about it all, and they could be bushwhacked just as soon as they left the doctor's house, but it seemed like their odds were better improved with the current plan.

It took some doing, but Chisenhall and Allison managed to talk Annie May into staying at Doc Griffith's. They felt she would be safer and better off there, and if the time came that they had to face down Hanley's thugs, she could be their backup at the doc's office. Well, her and Doc. Annie May didn't like the idea, but they had used logic and reasoning to convince her, and finally she gave in.

At daybreak Chisenhall and Allison started for the ranch, wary, not really expecting trouble, but alert to the possibility.

They hadn't gone far when Allison stated, 'You like my daughter, Annie May, don't you, John?'

Chisenhall smiled sheepishly. 'Guess I do, Jack. But you ain't gonna have to worry. No drifter like myself is going to take her away from you.'

'Why not? I don't have any objections to you, John. I was afraid you were just going to ride right out of her life and leave her hurting.'

'The thought had crossed my mind,' Chisenhall said coolly.

'What are you runnin' from, son? I doubt it's as bad as you think. I would hate to see you ruin your life over Hanley and those masked riders. But I will say that you did scare me, the other night at my spread. The way you cut down those riders. You plumb have got a darkness about you, son.'

'Jack, there's more to me. Somethin' I've been meaning to tell you, and right now I would like you to know. I've already told Annie May,' he paused. 'Now, I want you to know.'

'Hold up there,' Allison replied. 'Am I goin' to like this or not?'

Chisenhall smiled. The smiles were becoming a little less frequent of late, and it felt good to be able to flash one. 'Jack, you've been real good to me. I hope you don't look at me differently now . . .I'm just goin' to come right out and tell you that my. . . .'

Before he could finish that thought, Allison spoke. 'Your name's not John Hall.'

Chisenhall stopped and eyed the rancher. 'How. . . ?'

'Son, I've seen how you respond to that name, and I was sure that it wasn't your real one.' The rancher didn't seem angry. 'So, tell me what your real name is, and what happened to you.'

And Chisenhall told him the whole story, start to finish, or at least to where he was now.

'So the name's Chisenhall,' Allison said casually. 'I've heard that name somewhere. Nothing bad, mind you. I don't blame you for what's eating at you, son. You got more cause to hate Hanley than I do. That's for sure.'

It was plain as that. They drove the rest of the way in under-standably pleasant silence.

When they arrived at the farm, Rory Cabot hailed them from the barricade and the gate opened to allow them inside.

Allison sighed, for he had half feared that he would return to a smoking ruin or be ambushed by Hanley's men, killed on his own land.

When they were safely inside, Allison asked, 'Did you have any trouble, Rory?'

Rory looked very worn out. 'Yeah, a little.'

'Hell's bells, give it to me,' Allison said. 'How can it get any worse?'

Rory nodded. 'It can, and it is, Mr Allison. We lost a few of the men last night. They rode back to their families. They just up and left when the rest of them left last night.'

Allison sighed once again. 'Can't say that I can blame any of them.'

'So, our numbers are gettin' lower and lower,' Chisenhall noted.

'That they are.'

'How is Old Luke?' Rory asked.

'It doesn't look too good for him,' Allison replied. 'But he's one tough son-of-a-gun. He may just surprise us all and survive.'

'Well then,' Chisenhall said as he swung down from the wagon's seat, 'things can still get worse for him, and all of us.'

Rake Hanley shot the mangy dog through the head because it hadn't barked.

That was at least two times the yellow mutt had let his men ride back without announcing their arrival. A dog that didn't bark was like a gun that didn't shoot – it wasn't any worth to him. He had to have his precautions, and that started with the dog's barking.

The riders filed in just as Hanley put a second shot into the dead dog for good measure. He looked up from his entertainment and said, 'Pete, you are being a bit quiet. Don't tell me that one man managed to gun down a bunch of my men again.'

'I don't know what happened, whether it was one man or more, but someone sure as hell killed a lot of ours,' Pete Santee responded.

'At least you aren't spinning some tale of one man killing them all, as you told me the other night.'

'Like I said, I don't know exactly what happened. But those men I left out at the Allisons are all dead,' Pete added.

'It's a damn good thing I brought in new men just yesterday or you boys would have to work harder. I'm beginning to run low on money, men and whiskey, Pete. Let's just say I'm not a happy man right now.'

'We are doin' our best, Mr Hanley,' Pete said.

'Uh huh, just like Bish?' Hanley dropped his gun back in its holster.

Pete bit his upper lip gently. He did not say anything in response.

Hanley walked over to him and reached up to take hold of his stirrup. 'You know, I would hate to think I spent all this money on you boys, hard earned or not. . . .'

'You mean you stole the money,' Pete heard himself say suddenly, and also immediately regretted it.

'Damned right I stole it. What the hell does that matter? Think it's easy to rob banks and such? You know I didn't get it any other way.'

'You know I didn't mean anything by it, Mr Hanley,' Pete apologized.

The other riders had already dismounted. Hanley suddenly

grabbed Pete's leg and jerked him out of the saddle, spilled him into the dirt. He kicked Pete before he could stand. Pete thought about going for his gun, but he knew that would have been suicide. He knew Hanley was insane and that he had a better chance of surviving by taking a beating, than in a gun fight.

Hanley kicked him again, this time directly in the face.

Pete still did not get up. He just covered his face with his hands.

Hanley next kicked him in the stomach.

Pete tried to roll out of the way.

Hanley skipped toward him and kicked him in the ribs this time.

Pete suddenly lost his reserve. He came up with a bunch of dirt swinging. Hanley sidestepped and slammed a hard right into Pete's stomach. Pete blew out his breath with a loud groan.

Hanley kneed Pete between the legs, followed that with an uppercut into his jaw, and knocked him back to the ground in another burst of dust and dirt.

The other men had gathered around to watch. No one seemed the least bit interested in stopping the fight. They were men who minded their own business, unless there was money in it for them. There was. They had been hired and paid by Hanley to do what he wanted done, and they were promised considerably more. If he wanted to beat the hell out of one of his men – even his right-hand man – or kill that man, that was not their business.

If he paid them as promised. And of course, no one wanted to go up against Rake Hanley willingly. He was definitely crazy.

Pete tried once more. Swung a right.

Hanley took it on the outside of his shoulder and followed it with two quick, hard blows, right, then left, to both sides of Pete's face.

Pete then attempted weakly to kick Hanley, but Hanley caught his foot and jerked it over his head, busting Pete in the dirt.

Pete finally went for his gun. It was a surprisingly fast draw, but Hanley was faster. Pete realized that before his revolver cleared leather. He looked up to see Hanley smiling, looking down his long .44, looking down at Pete the same way he had looked at that mangy yellow mutt.

Hanley cocked the hammer back.

'Please – please, Mr Hanley. I wasn't thinking . . .'

'Yeah . . . that's a fact.'

'For Christ's sake, Mr Hanley. I lost my head for a moment. I've been ridin' most of the night. Please. I'm just tired.'

'I know. You've been holed up all night in my saloon, drinking my booze . . .'

'I didn't mean anything by it . . . please, please . . . I beg you. . . .'

Hanley spoke clearly and slowly. 'Put your gun away, Pete.'

'Please don't kill me, Mr Hanley,' Pete pleaded.

'Pete, Pete. I do like you. I don't want to hurt you.'

'Thank you, Mr Hanley.'

Hanley again spoke clearly and slowly. 'But if you don't put your gun away, I will blow a hole in your head.'

'Oh, sorry, Mr Hanley. I'm sorry. I wasn't thinking, that's all.' Pete reached the revolver back into his holster.

Hanley fired his gun, taking off half of Pete's head.

CHAPTER 20

THE FACE OF THE DEVIL

When night came about, Chisenhall and Allison sat down to a dinner of beans and hard cornbread, then they went out to the rounded barricade and called all the men, save the ones that were on guard duty, to gather around them.

Earlier that day Chisenhall had slipped caps on the nipples of his .44 revolvers and had packed charge and ball. He had also got cartridges for his new Colt from the box Doc Griffith had given him, and filled his gun belt and revolver, packing his pockets even. And now he had a double-barreled shotgun, too. Chisenhall reckoned this would be just the thing for close-in saloon shooting.

Allison also had a double-barreled shotgun, plus two revolvers, one in a holster, the other a .36 Navy in his belt. They were loaded, but as Allison had seen when Chisenhall had made just that statement as they armed themselves, there might be more men than they knew of.

'Now,' Allison began, 'I don't expect you men to follow me, not with the way things have been goin' like they have. Three more gone and all, but I do want to know if I got any among you that still feel like this farm is worth guardin'. I can't offer you any more money, 'cause there ain't any. But I'm askin' you to stay.'

'We ought to be goin' with you, Mr Allison,' Rory said. 'I can't speak for the other men, but I say if you ride in there, just the two of you, it's certain death for you both.'

'I'm out of options, Rory,' Allison said.

'Well then, I might as well ride with you,' Rory replied. 'I won't have it any other way, Mr Allison.'

'OK, Rory. We won't turn anyone away that wants to help. But the rest of you, I'm askin' that you all stay here and take care of the place for me. If we don't come back, you'll hear about it sure enough, and there won't be anything keepin' you here. As it is, we need you men here at this time.'

'Hey,' one of the guards yelled. 'We have company coming.'

'Lord Almighty,' Allison spat.

Chisenhall clambered up on a wagon and looked out over the barricade. 'Lord Almighty is right, Jack. Some of them coming are farmers and ranchers.'

'Thank you, Lord,' Allison said, taking a seat and feeling some relief.

'Rory,' Chisenhall said. 'Let's open those gates and welcome our guests.'

'That would be my pleasure,' Rory Cabot replied, and went for the gate.

When they had filed inside, ten of them in all, and all well armed and steely eyed, Allison said, 'I can't tell you how much this means to me, boys.'

One of the newcomers, a middle-aged farmer with a hook nose named Clay Curran, said, 'We couldn't rightly leave all this to you, Jack. Some of the other men may, but we wouldn't do that to you. You've been a good friend and neighbor, and we take care of our own out here. We let them take you under, we'll be next. You were certainly right about that.'

'One time I hated to be right,' Allison replied.

'I understand you, but you made your point.'

'Thank you,' Jack Allison said to the men.

'No, no,' Curran began. 'Thank you, Jack. We are simple ranchers and farmers, not gun fighters, but we are men, and we must fight for what we have built.'

'Exactly,' Chisenhall responded. 'Fight for what is yours. We are goin' to be facin' possible death, gentlemen. But we intend to give death hell first.'

The saloon had once been called 'The What Cheer House' and had had its share of rowdy patrons before Hanley took it over, but not like those men he brought to the newly renamed 'Dead Man's Hand Saloon', complete with a new sign that he had his boys hang up outside.

Rake Hanley sat at a table with cards in front of him, a glass of beer at his hand, and a cigar clenched in his teeth. He was wearing his tatty cavalry uniform, sabre and all. He had taken to leading the ruffians himself, as his right-hand men so far had been flops, and worse yet, he did not tolerate mistakes. This guy with the scar that he had heard about from the men had taken a large enough toll without getting mad and doing in a number of his own hands. From this point forward he was in charge and no more mistakes could be made. No more of this masked night rider business. He had the town well in hand now, and everyone knew it was his boys by this time, and so now it did not matter. Mesilla was his, and pretty soon the farms around it would also be his.

When he began his seizure of the town and farms, he hadn't wanted to expose himself when he could hire others to take the risks for him. It wasn't that he was a coward. He just wasn't stupid either. No, Rake Hanley was no coward. In fact, he wanted this guy with the half-moon shaped scar for himself. He would like to try his gun hand against a so-called crazed hombre like that.

Hanley was certain this Texas or New Mexican drifter, this

rider with the half-moon scar, would be no different for him than any other man. Actually, he had wanted to try his gun hand on the One-Eyed Kid, but they had split up before he had the chance. It would have been a hell of a lot better to have killed the other two and kept all the gold and money for himself. But gun hands like the One-Eyed Kid were hard to come across. They were not too bright either, at least some of them. They didn't ask questions, and they certainly didn't mind killing folks.

Hanley had tried to surround himself with just such men.

That is why he sat with his back to the wall when he drank or played cards, even in his own saloon with his paid-off men.

A man could never be too careful.

Hanley had cleaned up a pot when Brennan came in, kicking a farmer in front of him, finally grabbing the lanky man by the back of the neck and throwing him down on the bar-room floor.

'Would you shoot the hell out of him and be done with it?' Hanley asked. 'Some of us are tryin' to play cards here.'

'Mr Hanley, I've got some news for you,' the lanky farmer said with a nervous voice.

Hanley put down his card hand reluctantly, and leaning forward on his elbows, said, 'What's goin' on here?' He was speaking to Brennan, who was grinning like a cat that just ate a bird as he stood over the farmer.

'The man says he has some news for you. Something to do with the other farmers,' Brennan noted.

'Is that a fact?' asked Hanley.

'That's a fact,' the farmer said meekly.

'What's your name, mister?"

'Martin. Nat Martin.'

'Well, Mr Martin, I'm about to blow your head clean off your shoulders. Tell God I said hi.'

'Please, Mr Hanley, I do have some news for you,' Martin begged.

'Speak now or forever hold your peace.' Hanley got up from behind the table and walked toward Martin, his thumbs in his gun belt.

'The rest of 'em – the ranchers and farmers – some of 'em, anyway – they are working together now,' Martin whimpered.

'Seriously? That's all you have to say?'

'Wait, I have more to say. It's – it's just I don't want them to get hurt. I know most of those men,' Martin said near tears.

'No, you don't want me to hurt you is more of the case,' Hanley said. 'Isn't that right, boys?'

The men in the saloon murmured their agreement. Nat Martin said nothing.

Hanley's revolver seemed to magically appear in his hand. 'I said, isn't that right?'

'Please, don't, for my family, Mr Hanley. I don't want them harmed,' Martin pleaded.

Hanley mocked Martin. 'My family, Mr Hanley. I don't want them harmed.'

'My – my wife, she's gonna have a baby. I just want to . . .'

Hanley didn't appear to care. 'So you're wife is about to drop one, huh? Is that right, Martin?'

'Yeah.'

'Yeah? How about "Yes sir!"?'

'Yes sir!'

'A farmer's poor pregnant wife . . . like I care. Well, I don't. You see, I really like pregnant women, Mr Martin . . . if you know what I mean.' Hanley could see the fear in the man's face. 'Ain't that right, Brennan?'

'Yes sir, that's how you like 'em,' Brennan chimed in.

'Why, you ought to have seen the pregnant girl I had me down in Mexico. She was just about to burst. Pretty little thing, she was. She wasn't too happy to see me, and she put up a fight, but me and Brennan here and a few of the other lads' sort of convinced her into what I wanted.'

Martin looked up from the floor and exhaled hard: he knew

133

he was looking at the face of a real-life devil.

Hanley spoke first. 'I will tell you this, Martin. I like pregnant women. But I don't like brats. You see, there ain't gonna be any little Rake Hanleys runnin' 'round unless I want them to be. In fact, I like pregnant women, but only once. After that . . . well, let's just say once is enough . . . if you get my drift? That pretty little Mexican gal went and scratched me. I didn't like that, Martin. Not at the least.'

Hanley paced as he spoke.

'Now, if you have something important to tell me, I suggest you do so quick. My patience with you is runnin' out.' He leaned down to get close to the farmer. 'And it best be good information.'

'It is . . . it is. Just leave me and my family alone . . . please,' Martin again begged.

'Of course, Martin, of course. If this information is worthy of that, you and your family are fine.' Hanley slipped his revolver back into the holster.

Several of Hanley's men had risen from their places of loitering and were now standing around the groveling farmer, wicked grins on their faces.

'The others, the local ranchers and farmers,' Martin stuttered, 'they're joined up together, in a group. About ten of them all together.'

'Ten ranchers and farmers against me and my men, so?'

'No – no sir, Mr Hanley,' Martin whined. 'Four or five spreads and all their men.'

'Let's get their names, Martin. Brennan, get this man something to write with. I think a list will shed more light on what he's tryin' to say.'

'Why do you need their names?' Martin knew he had spoken out of turn. 'I mean, Mr Hanley, what does it matter?'

'Oh, it matters to me,' Hanley said, 'because I say it matters. You understand? Because I said so!'

Martin just looked at Hanley, could see the man tottering on the edge of sanity and insanity.

Brennan went away and came back with pencil and paper and dropped them on the floor so that Martin could not reach them.

'Go and pick them up!' Hanley ordered.

Martin started to stand, when Hanley with his boot pushed him back down. 'Crawl.'

Nat Martin, on hands and knees and starting to sob, suddenly sat down in a splay-legged fashion after retrieving the materials.

'Go on and write the names!' Hanley snapped.

Sobbing, Hanley began to write down the names of the ranchers and farmers who had banded together. 'I don't want any harm to come to my family, Mr Hanley. I just want my family . . . my wife . . . left alone. That's why I came here. If I write these names down, I want my family left alone.'

Hanley, letting him write, looked above Martin's head and at the men gathered around. He was smiling devilishly.

Martin finished writing the names, and Brennan took it from him, handing it to Hanley, who quickly looked it over.

'Thank you,' Hanley said. 'I'll just check them off and out, one at a time. No more askin' or offerin' money for these dirt farms. I'm takin' them from now on.'

Hanley stuffed the paper in his pocket. 'I'll be surprised if the others don't come crawlin' in here on their bellies too,' Hanley stated.

'Not all are a part of this, Mr Hanley, some decided against goin' up against you,' Martin said. 'They don't want no part of Allison or that gun man of his.'

Hanley frowned. 'This gun man, tell me more about him.'

'He is tall, pretty tough-lookin', and wears four revolvers. Quite a shot, too, from what I hear, anyways. And crazy when it comes to fightin', I was told. They say he rode down on a bunch of your men all by his lonesome, killed some and ran off the others. He's got this jagged scar on his cheek, looks like somethin' clawed him good or somethin' like that.'

'What about this Luke Cochran fella? I had my men pay him a visit not that long ago?'

'Well, he ain't dead, from what I heard,' Martin replied.

'Really?' Hanley said.

'From what I heard, yeah. He made it to Allison's place, hurt somethin' awful like, but he was able to get out there. You didn't have to go and do that to that old man, he wasn't any worry to you,' Martin stated.

'Where did you get all this newfound courage, Martin? What, not worried about your pregnant wife any more, huh? Unexpected courage . . .'

'No . . . no . . . please, Mr Hanley,' begged Martin.

'Good . . . that's what I like to hear.' Hanley lived on the man's fear. 'Now, you say Cochran made it out to Allison's?'

'Yeah . . . I mean, yes sir, that's what I was told, and they hauled him to the doc. Guess he may still be there,' Martin said.

'Martin, that old man was supposed to be a warnin',' announced Hanley. 'Guessin' they didn't take it that way?'

'Well, I can't speak for them other men, but I sure did,' Martin said. 'I did.' He sounded very excited, like someone who had finally done something correctly.

'How about these men on the list?' asked Hanley.

'They're comin' for you, Mr Hanley. I was with them earlier when they all decided to come for you. Me and some others walked out, didn't want any part in this. We just up and left. . . .'

'Yeah, yeah, you said that already.'

'Yes sir. Cochran was a might popular man, lot of folks got upset when you – I mean – when. . . .'

'Brennan,' Hanley said.

Brennan snapped to attention. 'Yes sir, boss.'

'I'm gettin' tired of this dirty farmer, take him out in the street and shoot him,' ordered Hanley.

'Wait! No!' Martin shouted. 'You promised – you said.'

'I made no promises to you, Martin,' Hanley said, 'and besides, I can do what I like. Take him out of here, Brennan. I have a game to finish.'

'Yes boss, sure thing, Mr Hanley,' Brennan said obediently.

Martin didn't even move, just hung his head. 'And my wife and child?' he asked.

'I will take good care of her, Martin, not to worry yourself,' Hanley said, and he walked back to his table.

Brennan reached down and grabbed Martin by the back of his shirt's collar. Other men each took an arm, and lifted Martin up on wobbly legs, and started hauling him toward the door.

'Remember,' Hanley said, 'I really like pregnant women, and me and the boys . . . well, you get it . . .the boys and me will make sure to keep your wife entertained. Should be a real good time.'

The fight had gone out of Nat Martin – what little there had been, was now completely gone. He was just dead weight to the men hauling him out of the saloon, his eyes glazed over and unbelieving.

'But . . . . but . . . I helped you,' Martin found a little strength to say.

'I appreciate that too, Martin, I will be forever grateful,' Hanley replied. He then focused on Brennan. 'Brennan, I changed my mind . . . hang this farmer. My head hurts and I don't fancy hearing gunshots right now. His whinin' has given me a headache.'

Brennan nodded. He and the other men dragged Martin outside, and the largest number of others followed them.

'Get a rope, one of you, there's one on my saddle, c'mon, will you?' Brennan called out to the men.

Back inside the saloon, Rake Hanley's attention was on the poker game. 'All right, who's deal was it?'

CHAPTER 21

THE MASQUE OF DEATH

When Rake Hanley finished a few more hands and had bellowed for the men outside to come inside, he shoved the cards away from him, and shouted to the bartender for another shot of whiskey and a beer. It came, and he swallowed the shot in one gulp and the beer in three more gulps.

'Did you get that dirt farmer strung up?' Hanley asked Brennan, who was snickering in response.

'That fella was kickin' like a mule,' Brennan said.

'You should have seen him kick,' echoed another of the men.

'I would have liked to have seen that, but my attention was on the game. I take things seriously, boys. Reckon we ought to go over to give the doc a visit. Check on his patient, Mr Cochran. What do you think about that, boys? Think the doc has him doing better about now?'

'I reckon he is,' Brennan said. 'And the doc didn't even come and visit us to let us know he was entertaining a guest. That is just plain rude.'

'That it is. I want to keep the doctor around, seein' as we tend to have a few cuts and scrapes and other injuries in our

138

line of work, but, well, my gut is tellin' me that he should get gut shot or cut just like Cochran to make sure my message is getting to them other boys Martin mentioned,' Hanley spoke without much emotion.

'We strung that farmer up good behind the sign, Mr Hanley. He hangs down just above the porch of the saloon.'

Hanley beamed at Brennan. 'You know what I like, Brennan. You do a job, nice and neat like.'

Brennan returned the beam.

'What you do that gets me riled up is your rudeness,' Hanley said out of the blue. Brennan looked confused.

'I'm sorry. . . .'

'You're sorry for what, Brennan?' Hanley demanded.

The man thought for a moment. 'I . . . I'm . . . sorry for. . . .'

'Not sayin' yes and no and addressin' me as sir?' Hanley said.

'Yes . . . sir, that's what I'm sorry for . . .' Brennan could see that Hanley was still waiting for him to get the message '. . . sir.'

Brennan wasn't beaming any longer. He knew Hanley was set off easily and for no obvious reason, and he had seen the result of this on numerous occasions. The results were not pretty.

Hanley, after a brief moment, grinned. 'Drink up, boys,' he finally said. 'Then we will go and see old Doc Griffith. The whole lot of us.'

Over at Doc Griffith's house-office, Annie May sat by the stove and read a book by its flames. She was reading about Prince Prospero's attempts to avoid a dangerous plague known as the Red Death by hiding out in an abbey. The Masque of the Red Death had always been one of her favorites. She wore jeans, a flannel shirt and boots, one leg thrown up over the arm of the chair in very unladylike fashion.

After a minute she put the novel down and rubbed her eyes – the room she was in seemed a different color each time she looked up from the book, much like the seven rooms of the abbey in the novel.

Doc Griffith came in from the back room and put a fresh pot of coffee on to boil.

'How's the book?' he asked Annie May.

'Well. . . .'

'Bored or tired with it?' the Doc replied.

'Just tired, I reckon,' she said.

'How many times have you read that novel? There's other books, you know!'

'No, the novel is wonderful . . . one of my favorites . . .I have a little cabin fever I reckon. With what happened last night and thinkin' about Pa – and Ro – I mean, John.'

'You don't have to pretend with me,' the doc said. 'I know his name ain't John. I don't know what it is, but it sure ain't John. When I met him, he'd just decided on that, spur of the moment type of thing. I could tell by the way he said it.'

'You think . . . well, you think the rest of the men are goin' to help out?' she asked.

Doc Griffith shook his head. 'It's hard to get men to do things like what your pa has asked them to do. Most of them fellas 'round here are good men, just not much for fightin' and bloodshed.'

'Is anyone?'

'Unfortunately, yes,' the doc replied. 'From what I hear, that fella of yours ain't half bad at it.'

'My fella?' she said in response. 'Least he has just cause.'

'He is your fella, ain't he? I mean, I seen the way you two eye each other,' Doc Griffith smiled. 'It's downright sickening . . .a bit.'

'I reckon he is my fella,' Annie May said.

'That sounded like you were sure,' the doc noted.

'Well, that's because I ain't.'

'Annie May, let me tell you something. That man's got something tearing him up from deep down inside of him. It's eatin' him alive. More aptly, it's killin' him. But it's a just sort of darkness, if there is such a thing. He won't be, least as I can tell, not ready for love till he's avenged himself.'

'You know more than you're lettin' on, Doc,' Annie May replied.

'Do you?'

'Yes, he told me everything.'

'Well, he wouldn't have unless he felt he could trust you, or he felt close to you. You don't have to know a man like him too long to see that,' the doc said.

Annie May nodded. 'I think I'm in love with him, Doc. I don't want to see him hurt.'

Doc Griffith put his hands on her shoulders. 'If there is anyone that can come through that kind of darkness, I reckon it's your fella.'

'Doc, I – wait, what is that? Do you hear something?'

Doc Griffith did hear something indeed. He turned away from Annie May and started for the window. Outside there came a sound like the hum of a beehive.

He peeked out the window. A score or so of Hanley's hired men were filing out of the saloon and walking down Main Street. Behind them, dangling like some sort of macabre scarecrow from the saloon sign, hung the body of Nat Martin.

CHAPTER 22

A HAIL OF BULLETS

'I don't know what exactly is goin' on, Annie May,' Doc Griffith said, 'but I have a bad feeling about this.'

Annie May slid out of her chair to come to the window and look out at what the doc was referring to.

'You should hide, I reckon,' said Doc Griffith, 'that way you can stay out of this. They don't need to know you're here.'

Annie May stopped pacing to speak. 'It looks as if they are heading here.'

'I reckon that's accurate, as I doubt those boys are out for a leisurely stroll down Main Street, and us being really the only other people in town, sort of makes it a given that I am their target,' the Doc reasoned.

'Think they know Old Luke is here?' Annie May asked.

'Most likely,' the doc replied. 'Probably comin' to finish the job.' He went over to the cabinet from which he had taken the holster he'd given to Chisenhall, and took out his revolver. He thought for a brief second before handing it to Annie May. 'Take hold of that and keep out of sight and be quiet. I don't want them boys to know you're here.'

Doc Griffith slipped into the room where Cochran was asleep and took a shotgun and rifle down from the rack on the wall.

When he returned to the room he said, 'Now, just sit tight. I'll handle this.'

'Doc!' Rake Hanley called at the house-office. 'Go on and send that old farmer out here. I got some unfinished business with that old coot. C'mon, send him out.'

The doctor went to the window, swallowed hard to build some courage. He opened the window a bit. 'Hanley, the only thing I would send to you is a ticket straight to hell. You come through my door and you'll be greeted with buckshot.'

'No need to get nasty, Doc. Just send out the old farmer and we'll leave you be; we won't bother you at all,' Hanley said.

'Like I would believe that, Hanley. Go to hell!'

'I didn't want to have to get rough with you, Doc. I kinda like you.' Hanley paused. 'But you asked for it.'

Brennan, at a nod from Hanley, moved toward the door. 'He's bluffin',' Brennan said. He stepped up on the porch and very carefully turned the knob.

Alan Brennan opened the door.

The blast from one of the barrels of Doc Griffith's shotgun tore Brennan's face away and launched him backwards out into the street. Brennan rolled once, twitched, and then was motionless.

Doc Griffith shouted, 'Who's next?'

The thugs on the street spread out in all directions, some hit the dirt, others dived behind barrels on the boardwalk behind them, and some hid behind posts.

Doc Griffith used the barrel of his gun to push the door back and then flipped the latch.

'Hanley, it didn't have to be this way,' Doc Griffith yelled.

Hanley was behind a post of the boardwalk directly across from the doctor's house-office.

'No, it didn't, Doc. I gave you a chance,' he yelled in reply. 'The hell with you.'

'You think you can hold us all off all by your lonesome, Doc?'

'He ain't alone,' Annie May shouted as she came to the window.

'Hush, girl,' snapped Doc Griffith. But it was already too late.

'Got yourself a girl, huh, Doc? That wouldn't be old man Allison's little brat, would it?'

'What's it to you?' Annie May shouted back.

'Annie May, you should've stayed hidden,' Doc Griffith began.

'No way, Doc. They'd find me soon enough, I reckon, after they rushed the place – besides, I could just as well be hit as I tried to hide once they start shooting up your place.' She turned back to the window and shouted. 'You boys come on towards the house and you'll find out just how well I can handle a gun.'

Already some of Hanley's thugs were working their way around the back of the building.

Doc Griffith said, 'That rifle there, that's all we've got, besides that pistol and me with a few rounds left for the shotgun.' He patted the shotgun fondly. 'We got to make sure that we don't go firing wildly. Make every shot count. I'm goin' to lock off this room by closin' that door to my bedroom. That should give us less to defend, don't ya think?'

Annie May nodded.

The doctor went to do what he said. Annie May kept a vigil by the window.

The rush came a few minutes later.

Two men ran directly at the house-office from across the street, sidled up against the building and tried to make their way toward the door. Three more went around the back. One started toward the back from the other side. Annie May lifted the revolver as he made his move, and fired, right through the window's glass, and caught the man in the left leg. He went down in the street clutching his leg and screaming in pain. Another shot from her revolver and he went silent – most likely forever.

They could hear wood splintering in the bedroom now. Someone was trying to break down the door, it would seem.

'This is not good, Annie May,' Doc Griffith said.

'You'd better get in the back with Old Luke. Barricade that room off too,' advised Annie May.

Doc Griffith darted off to do as instructed, and with all the strength he could find, managed to pick up the old man and carry him into the main room. He put him on the floor.

'What's happening, Doc?' Cochran asked.

'Hush and sit tight, Luke, you damn near gave me a hernia carrying you like I just did,' the Doc said.

Suddenly the darkness of the night was lit up with gunfire. Glass shattered and wood splintered. Bullets tore their way into the room. Annie May and Doc Griffith dropped to the floor.

'They'll rush us from the cover of these shots,' Annie May shouted.

'And we won't be able to stop them,' the doctor responded.

'I reckon not,' Annie May replied.

'No, I reckon not.' Already Doc Griffith was thinking of shooting Annie May to spare her from the horrors of what those men would do once they got to her.

They had ridden hard and fast, Chisenhall, Allison, Rory and the other ten volunteers. As they approached Mesilla gunfire could be heard. Lots of gunfire. Enough gunfire to make their hearts grow cold.

Chisenhall said, 'I say we divide our force, come in from two sides over just ridin' in as one large group. Least we'd get all shot up.'

'That's a good thought,' Allison acknowledged. He turned to the men. 'You, and you three, come with me. Chisenhall, you take the rest and cut down that side trail there. It will lead you to the opposite side of the street.'

'Sounds good,' Chisenhall replied, and he and the other four men, Rory among them, rode hard for the opposite side.

'C'mon, boys,' Allison said, 'Let's give 'em hell.'

The bullets tearing at the doc's house-office were ripping apart his books on the shelves. This made him sad. Things were jumping and falling every which way, but that one thing, the destruction of his books, that just was the icing on the cake.

The back door was heaving with the pressure of several men's shoulders, he guessed. The front door was too. A man's face appeared suddenly in the window, a hand lifting a revolver.

The face vanished amid a stream of blood when Annie May fired into it, catching the man unexpectedly in the forehead.

Doc Griffith rolled over on his back with a grunt, lifted the shotgun, and aimed at the back door and then fired. Wood splintered and flew in all directions, and he heard the toppling of bodies. He hurriedly shoved two more shells into the weapon.

More pressure on the door.

He fired another blast at the door and there was nothing heard from the other side this time.

There was a very large gap in the door as a result of his shots. It was big enough for a man to put his head through. Doc Griffith waited for the chance to shoot the man who dared to try.

Annie May lifted her hand and emptied her revolver into the front door. She could hear the thudding of boots racing out of the way.

She had driven back the assailants at least momentarily.

She reached up, took the rifle away from the wall where she had set it a while ago, and hit the floor once more. Keep low, she told herself. After making sure it was loaded, she gritted her teeth and raised the rifle. It was leveled on the front door.

This was the end, and she knew it, and she intended to make sure she took a few of the assailants with her before they took her and the two older men with her.

CHAPTER 23

ALL HELL
BREAKS LOOSE

Chisenhall, Rory and the three men with them came around the other side and then into the street during the long, loud volley of gunfire. Chisenhall's heart ached to hear it. He knew instinctively that it was Annie May and the doc under the barrage.

Hellbent for leather the five men rode, screaming at the tops of their lungs, trying to draw the attention of the attackers, and with bloodthirstiness on their minds.

And from the other side came Allison and the four men with him, right in the middle of the gun fight.

Annie May had once heard her pa say, 'When things got the worst, you need someone to ride the river with.' She always knew that meant someone you could trust or count on.

Annie May needed someone to ride this river with at that moment.

She lifted the old rifle, wishing really for more bullets for the revolver, but thinking, wishing ain't goin' to make it so. You make do with what you have.

At that very moment the door cracked open at the hinges and soared into the room.

This was the end, she thought.

Chisenhall balanced the shotgun against his hip as he rode, and when he approached the group of Hanley's thugs, he cut loose with one barrel, showering bits of shot and powder on their heads, but did not actually hit any of them.

Then the world seemed to come undone with the overwhelming resonance of more gunfire.

Allison had met Chisenhall and his riders in the middle, and Hanley's men were returning their fire with all that they had. Close quarter slaughter with shotguns and pistols.

Chisenhall witnessed one of Hanley's men spring up and grab Allison by his leg, pulling him from the saddle. Chisenhall rode by and clipped Hanley's man with the barrel of the shotgun, maneuvered back around and rode down on him as he tried to stand up, hitting him back with the horse.

That had given Jack Allison time to get back on his feet and get his pistol out of its holster and into his hand. He quickly shot the man in the side of the head.

'Much obliged,' he shouted to Chisenhall, but the horseback cyclone was gone, riding hard for the doc's house-office and the shattered front door.

After the door had been busted open, Annie May had shot the first man through right in the chest.

The doc let the shotgun rip and carried yet another of the assailants back and out of the doorway, and wounded another man in the process. But in the mêlée a shot from one of the attacker's guns had hit the ducking doctor and caused him to drop the shotgun to the floor. Another shot tore into his chest and he wobbled momentarily on his heels, and then fell to the floor.

The injured Luke Cochran, cognizant now, tried to skulk for

the fallen weapon, but the pain was plaguing his stomach and he was far too slow. He died from a shot to the head.

Annie May failed to drop another man before hands were on her, the rifle ripped out of her hands, and she was thrown violently to her feet, pushed hard against the wooden platform.

'We're goin' to have us some fun, little miss,' one of the men said, but there really wasn't much time to enjoy his comments.

A wild-eyed man rode into the room on a horse, creating a hole through one man who had loitered too long at the doorway. Then, dropping the shotgun, the wild man's hands became nearly unseen as he held two revolvers and took out the man who had spoken the words to Annie May.

And those two revolvers weren't done speaking, like roaring bears, and each time they spoke another man fell before their ear-splitting growl.

Meanwhile, out in the street, the gunfight had turned into a full-out war. Chisenhall took one look at Annie May, saw that she was alive and well – relatively – and that she was using one of the fallen thug's revolvers. He nodded at her, spun his horse, and rode back into the fray.

Hanley and a few of his men, about all that was left of his gang, were back-stepping toward the saloon, firing wildly as they did so.

Off his horse now, Chisenhall ran along the boardwalk. He was chasing them. Hanley, well trained in survival – as most rats were – had back-stepped in such a way that one man was almost directly in front of him, and one on each side.

Chisenhall's revolvers needed to be reloaded. He holstered them, and swift as a hiccup, the extra two in his belt appeared in his hands, belching fire.

The man on Hanley's left took his first shot in the collar and was knocked back into Hanley, who speedily seized the man and used him as a shield, dragging him along with him as he continued to walk backwards.

Chisenhall took the man on the right next. One clean shot. The man wheeled and fired his pistol into the boardwalk before falling lifeless. He had fallen on to his left arm then face first, the right side of his face missing.

One of the other men got off a shot that hit Chisenhall in the left shoulder and threw a stream of blood from the hole.

The shot merely knocked Chisenhall off balance a bit. He went down on the boardwalk to one knee, rapidly fired off another few shots at his attacker, and hit him once in the torso, about his waist. The man crumpled, clutching the wound.

Hanley had been sending slugs at Chisenhall hastily, but the tall stranger seemed to have luck on his side. The bullets hit all about his location, but never actually hit him.

Chisenhall pushed himself up, leaned against a storefront for support, took aim, and shot through the dead man Hanley used as a shield. The blast ripped into the man's chest, went clear through and tore into Hanley's side.

With a shriek, Rake Hanley dropped the man and dived headlong through the batwings into the saloon.

Calmly, Chisenhall took a bandanna from his pocket and slipped it beneath his shirt to plug the bullet wound. The bullet, he was certain, had gone entirely through.

Luck was indeed on his side.

As if ambling to church on a Sunday morning, Chisenhall made his way toward the saloon. In the moonlight, the scar on his face was clearly illuminated.

The sound of gunfire had gone from the streets of Mesilla. The only men left standing were Allison's and, as usual, the town folks had stayed well within their homes – though there were few of them to begin with. Allison thought it disgusting, but then maybe, this was a step toward a new start.

A few of the men had helped the injured Doc Griffith up on his platform, and in their own way, were doing their best to make him comfortable. He was hurt bad, but still alive.

'Chisenhall's going to the saloon all by himself,' Rory Cabot said running into Doc Griffith's ruined office.

'No one can stop him,' Annie May said solemnly. 'He's got to settle the score.'

'I reckon,' Allison said, 'that's right. I promised him he'd get his chance.' And with that said, Jack Allison directed a couple of the men to cover the back of the saloon. 'We don't want that snake escaping, do we?' The two men darted to the back of the saloon.

'Not much of a chance for him,' Rory said, watching as the lamps died in the saloon, pitching the inside into darkness. 'Hanley's leading him into a trap, I suspect.'

'Chisenhall has to do this alone,' Allison replied. 'I don't like it any more than you all. But if he doesn't do this by himself, he will never quench his thirst for vengeance.'

CHAPTER 24

SEE YOU IN HELL

Ross Chisenhall stopped just before the batwing doors of the saloon. He gathered his strength and nerve before calling out, 'Hanley, I want you to know just who the hell I am.'

'I don't give a rat's. . . .' Hanley began to yell back.

'I was left for dead. Buried alive, like some animal. Only I wasn't dead. I came back for you, Hanley.'

'Good, you can eat my lead, you crazy fool!' Hanley shouted. 'Come on in and I'll make sure you stay dead this time. I guarantee you won't come back a second time.'

'Or I just might, Hanley,' Chisenhall spoke calmly and clearly. 'Vengeance will be mine. In this life or the next. There is no escape for you. My name is Ross Chisenhall, and you cut my face and buried me alive. But . . .' his blood was rising now '. . . not before killin' my boy!'

A slight laugh was heard from inside. 'You're that farmer? Seriously?' Hanley said.

'No, you killed that farmer,' Chisenhall replied. 'I'm a different man now. I'm a killer now.'

And with that Chisenhall jumped through the door landing on his belly.

Two bright orange bursts lit up the back of the saloon,

152

showing Hanley's face for a brief second or two.

That was long enough. Chisenhall clipped a shot at him, but heard it hit the wall behind. He could hear Hanley scrambling, knocking over furniture. He fired another shot in the direction of the sound, and then heard the telltale sound of a bullet hitting flesh and bone.

He heard Hanley scream, 'Damn you!'

Chisenhall rolled from his location just before two slugs ripped up the floor where he had been. Chisenhall was now at the edge of the long wooden bar, his eyes slowly adjusting to the darkness.

He could make out the outlines of an overturned table and chair near the other end of the bar, and he felt confident that was the spot the shots had come from.

Carefully he raised one of his revolvers and took aim at the center of the table, fired, and heard a loud grunt, and witnessed a form roll from behind the overturned table to the foot of the bar.

'Damn, you got me again,' Hanley admitted. 'You got me good – but I reckon that wound of yours ain't doin' you no good either.'

'I'll live,' Chisenhall said, not knowing that to be the truth. He was feeling the pain of the bullet wound and he was getting weaker from the loss of blood. The blood had been dripping slowly out and down his arm, pooling at his elbow, and soaking through his shirt in a large, wet patch.

'I tell you somethin', farmer. . . .' But Chisenhall never heard the rest of what Hanley was about to propose, as he suddenly pulled himself upright, and using his injured arm, palmed up on the bar and pulled himself toward Hanley.

Hanley unexpectedly caught on to the trick and pulled himself up to shoot at Chisenhall. But the former farmer had been quicker and rammed two slugs into the bar just in front of Hanley, sending splinters of wood flying into Hanley's face, not hurting him, but halting his shots.

Hanley made a crouched run across the length of the saloon, and from his perch, Chisenhall managed to shoot again, missing Hanley as he tripped over his own feet and went down in a pile.

Hanley next rolled on his back, and looked past his own feet, fired a few shots at Chisenhall. One of the shots unfortunately hit Chisenhall in the upper thigh and knocked him back into the bar, crashing some bottles to the floor. His hand was forced back at the shock and a shot smashed into the mirror behind the bar. Whiskey and glass rained down on him. Chisenhall found himself seated on the floor.

He scowled, forcing himself up on to a knee. Somehow a beer keg had been punctured and beer poured out, running like his bleeding shoulder wound.

Managing to get to his feet, Chisenhall stood, albeit on unsteady legs. He found it hard to move thanks to his thigh wound. He was crouching just enough to take the edge of the bar in for protection.

Another shot from Hanley's gun went over his head. Hanley then scrambled behind another table and he pulled a second one in front of the one he was behind.

Hanley raised his head abruptly and fired again. His shot missed Chisenhall, but just barely. He fired once more, only this time the gun clicked. He was empty.

Hanley panicked and threw the pistol at Chisenhall.

Chisenhall stood up behind the bar and stepped out, and limped painfully toward Hanley's position.

Hanley raised up his hands from behind the table.

Chisenhall ignored his surrender and kept coming.

When Chisenhall stopped directly in front of the tables, revolver leveled, Rake Hanley stood to meet his opponent. He was trembling.

'Take me to the nearest lawman,' he said. 'I give up.'

The grin on Chisenhall's face was as cold as a blizzard's blast, the eyes, even in the darkness of the saloon, were like the eyes of a demon.

Slowly he raised the revolver and shot Hanley in the leg.

Clutching the wound and screaming, Hanley fell back to the floor in pain.

Chisenhall shuffled agonizingly toward him and held the revolver over the fallen man.

'On your feet, you scumbag,' he said. 'Hanley, I want to see you fall.'

'It's over, I surrender,' Hanley pleaded. 'Please.'

'I said, on your feet!'

Rake Hanley rose slowly and excruciatingly to his feet – and then the sword was freed from its scabbard and cutting through the air toward Chisenhall.

Chisenhall managed to catch the sword swing with his weapon, coiled with his arm, and pulled the sword from Hanley's hand, sending the blade back and completely through one of the overturned tables.

'You're right,' he said. 'It is over.' He raised the revolver to Hanley's head.

And it clicked as Hanley closed his eyes.

Opening them swiftly, there was hope now in his eyes, and Hanley went for the sword.

Chisenhall stuck out his leg – the undamaged one – and Hanley tripped and went down in a heap, clutching for the table, but causing the table to topple upright, the sword blade sticking straight up like a tent pole.

Hanley pulled the sword out with a swift motion and swung wildly at Chisenhall.

Dropping the empty revolver, Chisenhall tried the other, but it too was empty. He dodged the sword's blade but not Hanley's fist that followed it. The blow caught him on the jaw and knocked him off his feet.

Hanley grabbed at the table, hobbling along, but Chisenhall was quick and reached out, caught Hanley's boot and yanked, bringing the man down hard, face first.

Chisenhall swarmed over him, grabbed Hanley's hair and pulled up his head, and drove it down into the floor hard. One time, then again. He heard bone breaking in Hanley's nose, but when he raised the man's head preparing to smash it for a third time, Hanley reached back with an arm and pushed Chisenhall away.

Both men, wounded and exhausted, wavered to their feet. Both bloodied.

Hanley kicked feebly at Chisenhall.

Chisenhall caught the boot again, pulled it up high, and Hanley in turn fell on his butt to the floor.

Hanley caught a chair, and in one motion used it to get to a knee and swung it at Chisenhall.

The chair crashed into Chisenhall's shoulder and part of his back, but he fell on Hanley. The two men did not fall to the floor this time, however.

Hanley had Chisenhall in a bear hug, applying what strength he had left. But though there was plenty of rage, there wasn't much strength.

Chisenhall countered by grabbing Hanley by the throat with one hand, and by the leg with the other. He lifted the man a bit off the ground, and pushed him back.

Hanley seized the sword once more, and as he went to thrust it toward Chisenhall he found himself being pushed down from the back toward the blade of the sword.

The point of the sabre easily went through his body, and it ended his life.

Chisenhall stumbled back from the skewered Hanley, watching as the man stumbled about desperately trying to free himself from the blade, as blood poured from the wound. And then he fell, landing in a semi-kneeling position, the point of the sword visible from the back.

The life in his eyes began to fade.

'See you in hell,' Hanley spat.

CHAPTER 25

LOVE, WONDER AND UNFINISHED BUSINESS

An hour became a day, a day became a week, and a week fell into a month.

Chisenhall convalesced at Jack Allison's ranch along with Doc Griffith, who was as ornery as ever. The place was now without a barricade, surrounded only by pastures, fields, pines, and the unfeeling, bleak hand of winter.

Chisenhall's wounds, though not completely mended, were improving, and the time that Annie May had dreaded, and in a way, the time that Chisenhall had dreaded as well, had come.

Annie May wore a dress that day. It was the only time Chisenhall had seen her wear one, and he was pleased with the results.

Chisenhall had saddled his horse, and the two of them walked to the barn, Chisenhall leaning on his horse. They walked unhurriedly, trying not to rush. It was about an hour till sunup, yet the sky was black as night. Thunder crashed. Lightning flashed.

After a minute, they stopped. Chisenhall dropped the reins to the horse, and they embraced. There were plenty of tears in Annie May's eyes.

'Do you have to?' she asked.

He said nothing, only nodded.

Drops of rain started to fall on them, like tears themselves.

'It began on a day like this,' he said. 'That feels so long ago now.'

'Then leave it there, in the past. It was a long time ago.'

He shook his head.

'You aren't even sure where to start looking,' she pleaded.

'One of Hanley's men told me some information about the man with the crazy eye. He said he'd gone south, probably to Mexico.'

'Mexico is a big place, I hear.'

'It is. But I will find him.'

'You could stay a little longer.'

Chisenhall smiled. 'I know. I wish I could. I do care for you, Annie May. You know once I finish this . . . I will. . . .'

She raised a finger to his lips. 'Don't make a promise to me. At least one that you cannot guarantee you will be able to keep.'

He pulled her to him, and they held each other as the rain grew stronger and dampened her hair and rolled off his hat.

'I will be back.'

He pulled away from her with some effort, took hold of the horse's reins, and swung up in the saddle. He turned to look out across the fields toward the thick pine forest. A bright flash of lightning illuminated the whole area. In that brief flash Chisenhall's revolvers picked up the light and seemed to shine brighter than ever.

Then the darkness came again, as it always did with Ross Chisenhall. Annie May took hold of his boot and looked up, the rain drenching her now.

He smiled down at her, and she returned it.

'Please, don't go,' she said softly.

'I don't have a choice, I really don't.'

'You do.'

'It's left undone, Annie May. There's still a couple of them left. If I leave it like this, it will haunt me for the rest of my life.'

'I will share that burden with you.'

He shook his head.

'I cannot ask that of you.'

'You don't have to.'

He looked her in the eye. 'I will return.'

'I will wait.'

He reined the horse away from her before there was a change of his mind, and rode hard and fast for the forest.

Annie May watched until he had disappeared on the horizon. Lightning flashed and it revealed an emptiness for her. Then there was darkness, and nothing was visible.

She wondered if she would ever see Ross Chisenhall again.